SEEDS OF DAWN
Volume Three

Redemption

Absolution

JAMBREA JO JONES

Seeds of Dawn Volume Three
ISBN # 978-1-78184-572-1
©Copyright Jambrea Jo Jones 2012
Cover Art by Posh Gosh ©Copyright 2012
Interior text design by Claire Siemaszkiewicz
Total-E-Bound Publishing

Published in 2013 by Total-E-Bound Publishing, Think Tank, Ruston Way, Lincoln, LN6 7FL, United Kingdom.

REDEMPTION

Dedication

Kim and Rhonda — Peter and Grey thank you. If not for the two of you pushing, they wouldn't exist. This book is for you. Susan, thank you for Greycen's name, spelled a little different, but it's for you. And Ive, you kick ass. I hope you enjoy your fictional man and the redemption of the Ice Queen.

To Sue for holding my hand through the hard parts and crying with me.

And as always — to Joy.

Chapter One

"I may be going on this trip to help out, but make no mistake about it, I'm not here for you." Peter Tyler declared to Greycen Sheppard before stepping on to the plane.

Damn his alpha for pairing him up with Grey on this rescue mission to save the missing pack members who'd left for Africa not so long ago. The pack needed to stop with the matchmaking. Peter would never have a mate. That had been beaten into his head time and time again by his family. He was an abomination no matter what Russ—the pack leader—or the others said.

Who cared if he thought Grey was hotter than hot with his bright blue eyes and shaved head? Who cared if every time he was in touching distance of the man, he wanted to wrap himself around that thick muscular body and fuck for days?

I do. That's who.

He desired Grey more than he really cared to admit—even to himself. But he wasn't playing into the whole mating thing. He'd help Grey get his sister, Ive, back and that was it. He was here to protect Grey — no, not that, he was here to retrieve the other pack members. Yes, that was his goal and if he watched over Grey while doing it, that was his business and no one else's.

"Whatever you say, man. I'll let you have your way for now because I'm worried about Ive, but after this little trip is over, you and I will be having a serious talk."

Peter jumped out of the seat he'd just got comfortable in to confront Grey.

"Who the hell do you think you are? I mean, really? All you want is a piece of ass and I seem to be handy. I've already told you — fags don't get mates."

"You keep telling yourself, sweetheart."

Peter moved closer and loomed over the Grey, one of the advantages of being so freakishly tall.

"We're gay and I'll say it one more time so listen closely. We. Don't. Get. Mates. Mating is for breeders. Didn't you get the memo?"

Peter shouldn't have been as worked up as he was, but he hated the ache in his chest when he was near Grey and it pissed him off no end that the fox shifter was so casual with his sexual orientation.

"I don't know who screwed you over, but you have a lot of learning to do." Grey glared up at him, not backing down an inch.

God he was sexy. Peter leant down and nipped at Grey's lips in a show of aggression. Grey growled and opened his mouth as if expecting a kiss. The two breathed in and out, neither moving to break whatever spell they were under. Grey licked his lip and stared into Peter's eyes.

The captain's voice interrupted their pissing match.

"Please buckle in. We're getting ready for take-off."

Peter backed away and moved as far from Grey as he could get. He'd started to shake and needed to sit down. Confrontation wasn't his thing, but something about Grey seemed to bring it out of him.

Grey cleared his throat like he was getting ready to say something. Peter glared at him. He was done talking for now. He'd focus on what Bella, the Masters' pack seer, had told him. It wasn't much to go on. Joy, one of the four-member team who had been sent to Africa in the first place to dispose of an evil vessel that had taken over another shifter, had magically activated a necklace, flashing out a distress call. The team consisted of Joy and her mate Zareb, along with Ive and her mate Djimon. Djimon was the one who had been infected with the Vessel. It was a long boring story that he didn't know all the details to, just what he'd heard.

Bella had said Ive and Djimon had been separated from Joy and Zareb. They were being sent to the location Bella had pinpointed from the images. Ive and Djimon had gone off map. Bella had said it was as if they had disappeared, but weren't dead because somehow she would have known. He really should have paid more attention.

Peter had no idea what they would find when they got there. He hoped it wasn't the corpses of pack mates. He could handle just about anything, but not dead bodies. He'd seen enough of those to last him a lifetime.

Not wanting to think about his past, he moved his gaze to Grey—the one thing he could look at for days. The man was built with muscles everywhere. His reddish hair had been buzzed close to his head and Peter thought he'd glimpsed a tattoo or two when they'd shifted for their last run.

Looking wasn't the problem. Taking action was.
Hell, he knew what to do. He'd just never had the
chance to experience it. Sex wasn't an option for him.
When he'd first figured out he was gay, he'd been
scared shitless. Fifteen and knowing he wanted cock
not pussy wasn't something he'd relished figuring out
when people were killed for less in his pack.

And now he was back to thinking about things
better left buried. Until Grey had shown up he'd been
able to lead a pretty normal life. Russ, the pack
Master, had accepted him when he'd asked to join the
pack. He was never left to feel unwanted. His hand
was a perfect companion. He didn't need sex, not
when he had a family again. One who seemed to love
him for just being him.

"Are you going to sit there and brood the whole way
to Africa? If so, it's going to be a long trip."

"I'm not here for your amusement," Peter huffed.

"I know. If you were, I'd have your lips wrapped
around my cock right now and you'd let me mark
you."

Peter's jaw dropped in astonishment. *He did not just
say that.* Who was he kidding? Grey had said it and
meant it. If Peter was man enough he'd go take what
he wanted and damn the consequences, but there was
no way he'd risk Grey's life for a quick fuck or suck.

He'd seen what had happened to other gay shifters
and it wasn't pretty. He was lucky to be alive. Nope —
he'd stick with his palm. People didn't get killed for
jackin' off.

The plane started its assent and Peter did his best to
ignore Grey.

"I can't believe my sister went off half-cocked to
follow some guy all the way across the planet." Grey

knew his disgust was coming through loud and clear, but he was jealous of the fact that his sister had a mate that might just love her back, once he'd come out of his possessed fog, while Grey was stuck with someone who fought him every step of the way.

He enjoyed a good fight and makeup sex as much as the next guy, but Peter took things to the extreme. Maybe he needed to ask Russ, the Master's alpha, what Peter's story was. Peter wasn't talking. Every time Grey tried to get him alone, Peter would bolt.

"Why wouldn't she? I mean, really, who wouldn't want to follow their mate if they were allowed to have one?"

Peter's wistful tone gave Grey pause. Why couldn't the other man see that it was possible and that his mate was standing right here beside him ready to start their lives together? But no, Peter pushed him away again and again.

* * * *

The two disembarked the plane. Africa was beautiful, so lush and brilliant. The sun was setting and the scenery was bathed in gold and orange through the green of the jungle. Grey didn't think they had a name for where they had landed. At least not that he saw on any maps. He stretched to get the kinks out. The flight had been uncomfortable for many reasons. One being that Peter had refused to talk to him after their encounter. Damn the pilot for interrupting. Things could have got interesting. Peter needed to loosen up. Or Grey should get them locked in a room together somewhere. That could be an idea for when they were finished here.

When Russ had told them they needed to come to Africa, Grey had been ecstatic thinking of all the time he and Peter would have to talk so they could figure out where they should go from here, but Peter had read or slept the whole way, completely ignoring Grey.

He was all for staying in Peter's pack. He had no desire to go back with the other foxes. He'd be happier with the wolves and he figured that's where his sister would want to be as well. Or, hell, they could all go start their own tribe somewhere. Not that Vivian would come. Her mate was the Master's alpha. Who'd known when he was sent to follow the princess of the fox's den that he'd be leaving his home for good, but good riddance. He only stayed there because his sister, Ive, and his charge, Vivian the princess, were content at home. Once Ive and Vivian had sneaked away, he knew the time for change was upon him. Now, both the women had mates and so did he. It should be a happy time in his life, not a frustrating one. And to top it all off—first they had to go save the day.

They'd have to sleep in the plane tonight—it was getting dark and there was no way Grey wanted to traipse through the jungle at night. His fox form was small and compact, like his human form, and he didn't want to risk unknown predators.

"We should sleep—get a good start in the morning."

"I agree. The pilot said we're about a day's walk from the coordinates Bella gave him. Not that we'll be able to pick anything up. Why the hell didn't Russ send a magic user?"

"No clue, but it was his call and we go with it. We can shift if we have to and track that way. Shouldn't be too hard."

"Whatever, man. I'm really not tired, but we should try to rest up. I want to leave at first light. Maybe eat something."

Grey looked back at where Peter stood at the base of the steps leading to the plane. He was so tall and lean and — yeah — Grey needed to stop thinking sexual thoughts or he'd embarrass himself. He was surprised Peter was talking and it must have shown on his face.

"What?" Peter put his hands on his hips and glared.

He wanted to climb Peter like a monkey and do dirty things. He was getting hard.

Peter sniffed the air and his face turned a brilliant red.

Fuck.

Stupid pheromones.

Peter didn't wait for an answer. He turned and marched up the steps leading to the aeroplane. Great, he'd fucked up again, but he couldn't help the way his body responded to his mate's. They were meant to be together and his fox couldn't understand the separation. Grey growled and followed Peter into the plane. He was unsettled. Something about this place had him on edge, on top of his personal problems. They needed to find the other shifters and get out of there.

He knew Ive had to be fine. They were bonded and if she died or were hurt he'd feel it deep in his soul. He already had one hole there, he didn't need another one.

"We'll find them." Peter assured him from his seat.

Grey had no idea how Peter did that. It was like the wolf could read his mind. It was a little disconcerting. He nodded and continued on to a seat across the way. No matter how friendly Peter might act at times, Grey didn't think he'd appreciate him sitting down next to him.

He had to prove that he didn't just want to fuck Peter. That was going to be hard because he wanted his mate in the worst way. It was almost painful for him not to complete the bond.

Shit. Things couldn't get worse—could they?

Chapter Two

All hell broke loose. Ive Sheppard didn't know what was going on. One minute she was taking a break from the heat, watching her companions do some magic thing, and the next she was surrounded by natives yelling at her. She was getting soft. She should have heard something before they were overtaken. She was a shifter and a protector. Good thing her friend and charge wasn't here.

It wasn't like she expected the plane flying her, Zareb, Joy Rockwell and Djimon to crash. Or the pilot to die. Or to be lost in an African jungle. It should've been a cake walk. Get rid of the Vessel, that evil soul-sucking abomination that had caused so much trouble in the Master's pack house and the thing that had taken over her mate, causing him to do unspeakable things without his knowledge. Then they were to go back to the Master's pack house where she would get to know her mate, Djimon. Help him heal from being possessed by the evil Dmitri. The Vessel was the cause of it all. It possessed dark magics that suppressed a body's soul so another entity could take over. They hadn't discovered if the creature Dmitri was a demon or just a spirit gone bad. They might never know.

Now she was being hauled away.

"Let me go. What are you doing?" Ive screamed.

She struggled when she saw Zareb and Joy go down. They couldn't be dead. Oh, God. Dji, her mate—he had to be okay, right? Fate couldn't be that much of a bitch. The man was so weak from the fight to gain control of his body and there was no way he could withstand this onslaught. She looked over and she was right. Dji screamed something in a foreign language and passed out.

Why were they taking her and leaving Joy and Zareb? It didn't make any sense. Nothing did. They picked up three packs and headed into the jungle. Ive continued to make a racket.

She didn't know why. It wasn't like anyone could help her now. It was her duty to be strong. If need be she would put herself in the line of fire. The most important things were the survival of her mate and the destruction of the Vessel.

Ive needed to pay attention to her surroundings. It wasn't like she had any magic. The other three would have been more suited to be the saviour of this little operation, but it was up to her.

In her heart of hearts, she might wish her brother was there to help, but she was happy Grey was far, far away because if she had to die Ive didn't want him to feel it. She dug her feet into the ground, making a small trail, but she stopped fighting. For now.

She couldn't understand a word being spoken. It had to be Afrikaans. She really needed to learn the language. If she'd known more about her mate before her and Vivian—her friend and the princess of the fox den—had run to the wolf compound, she would have taken the time to learn the language.

As it was, the vision had caused her and Viv to run before they were ready. Then Viv had got hurt and their lives had been go, go, go. Nothing was certain and, for an orderly anal person such as herself, it was pure hell.

Ive lost focus, everything looked the same. She would never be able to get back to Joy and Zareb. She and Dji were on their own and, right now, he wasn't going to be of any help. Just who were these people? Shit. Were they just locals pissed off because the group was on their turf or was it more than that? Could the evil that was Dmitri have come back to take over Dji again? Wouldn't Dji be more powerful in his homeland? Was Dmitri from here too? There were too many unanswered questions for her liking.

This would be on her terms, as much as she could make it. Ive stood up straight and held her head high. She might not be of royal blood, but she could damn well put on a good show.

The man who had dragged her through the jungle was trying to speak to her and shaking one of the backpacks at her. Like she could answer him. Ive glared, trying to stare him down. He could stand there all bloody day, but she still wouldn't be able to answer. Her only hope on that front was if Dji woke up. God, he'd be so confused. It was bad enough he was so down on himself. He couldn't have stopped the Vessel's possession.

Men could be so pigheaded sometimes. Taking all the blame when there was none, and it was worse when the guy had a hero complex. Dji was very old school in so many ways. Ive just wished he would wake up and do some magic mojo to get them out of there.

The slap came out of nowhere. Ive saw stars. What the hell? It wasn't like she could rub her cheek, either. They'd tied her hands and had her on a rope lead. Did they really believe she'd run into the unknown? Right now it was better to stick with someone who knew the terrain.

What was with her screwed-up luck? Could nothing go right?

The tribe guy continued to wave the bag around. When she still didn't answer he hit her harder. That totally wasn't helping! She moved her jaw around. It didn't feel broken, but she didn't know how much more hitting she could endure. Fuckin' bastards. If she'd had her hands free she'd have clawed their eyes out to make them wish they'd never taken her.

She wasn't expecting the sucker punch to her stomach. She doubled over and then he threw an uppercut that Ive could see coming from her hunched over position. As much as she wanted to back away, there was no way it was happening. It clipped her chin and she flew back, hitting the ground—then nothing. The blackness seeped in.

Djimon snapped out of his self-imposed trance when he saw Ive go down. He roared and tugged at his captors, charging the man who'd dared touch what was his. He started to shift when a wall of magic cut him off.

"*Genoeg.*"

The word echoed through his whole body and he stopped in his tracks. They were speaking Afrikaans, his native tongue, but who were these people and why was the old one telling him 'enough'? They should know better than to harm someone's mate.

"*Dmitri, wat is fout met jou? Hoekom is jy optree op hierdie manier, ons prober om jou te help.*"

"What's wrong with me?" Dji was trying to figure out why this man was calling him Dmitri and how he was trying to help him by beating on Ive.

He may have been out of it—that's right—Dmitri, the soul who'd possessed his body for so long. They thought—this wasn't good. Could he pretend? He might be able to, he'd lived with Dmitri inside him for so long, but he hated that spirit and thought he was through with him. That's what this trip was all about—get rid of the damn Vessel and start a new life.

"English, old man. What is the meaning of this?" Dji stood taller and shrugged off the hands holding him, letting the arrogance he remembered from Dmitri take over, and Dmitri didn't like to speak in Afrikaans, which was why he'd taught this tribe of renegades English.

"Dmitri, we saved you. This woman," the old man spat on the ground towards Ive. "She held you captive and has the sacred instrument we need and won't tell us where it is. The one you told us we would have back one day. That is why you are here, yes? It is time."

Dji closed his eyes but, when he did that, flashes of the past hit him hard and he fell to his knees. Blood and bodies, so many dead and it was all his fault. He couldn't do this. He was Djimon the protector of his tribe and he'd let them down.

"She doesn't speak our language and who are you to touch my woman that way?" Dji opened his eyes and demanded.

"I am the tribe shaman and I am to help you create more soldiers to take over the world. Why are you being this way, Dmitri? What has she done to you? She did not say she was yours." The old man pointed at Ive.

"Don't touch her again, or I will rip you apart."

"You are not yourself, sire."

"No, I'm not and stop calling me Dmitri or sire."

"What is the meaning of this?" the shaman demanded.

Power surrounded Dji and it wasn't of his own making. If he'd had better control of himself, this puny magic user would have never been able to get the drop on him. Here he was wallowing and it was happening again. People would die and it would be his fault.

"I am the protector Djimon and you will release us now."

"Dmitri warned us of this. You have taken back over? We will fix that. Where is the Vessel?"

It was Dji's turn to spit, right into the shaman's face, and he was slapped for his efforts. He growled. Dmitri would never take over again. Dji would kill them both first.

"You will never have the Vessel. It will be destroyed and you will be nothing. I will see to that, old man."

"Brave words for a man who is so weak. I should have known right off you were not Dmitri. Bring them both."

One of the old man's henchmen picked Ive up and threw her over his shoulder. Dji growled. They touched what was his and he would have none of it. Power swirled inside him, starting in a small ball working its way up and up—his fingertips tingled. It was time—his magic was coming back and ready to burst, the release—he needed it now. Then it was cut off again. Fuck.

"We'll have none of that, Djimon." The wall of magic was back and it moved around him, tightening more and more until he was trapped.

Dji threw his head back and howled. No—not again, never again would he be held captive. He drew from an inner strength he didn't know he had. Some reserve that had helped him to break free from the evil spirit. There was a man on each side of him and he ripped his arms out of their hands and grasped their wrists, tugging them around until he knocked them together—hard.

He was going for the shaman. If he took him down he could get his magic back—the power still constricted him, making him move like he was wading through water. He was so close he could almost touch the old man. Looks were deceiving—the shaman appeared brittle with wrinkles upon wrinkles covering his body and face, but the outstretched hands were enough for Dji to bounce off and hit the ground.

No. No, no, no, no, no!

He slammed his fist into the earth, using the dirt and essence from the land—anything that would help him to break the magical hold. Again, things were out of his reach and he hated having no control over his destiny. A new, primitive energy surged through him, but it wasn't enough. Once his power was blocked he couldn't get out of it. Not now when his strength was at its lowest.

"Do not worry. Dmitri will be back soon and you can sleep until you can be returned to the Ancients."

They must not have trusted him to stay calm because someone brought out twine and wrapped it around his throat and wrists—if he made one wrong move he'd choke himself. He would have to reserve his powers and not fight anymore. There had to be a way out of this. He might die, but he needed to save Ive.

Chapter Three

Grey woke up grumpy. His neck hurt from the uncomfortable plane seat and Peter was nowhere to be found. That shouldn't have surprised him in the least. The second Grey got too close, Peter ran away like he was on fire. He sat up and rubbed his shoulder. It wasn't helping. He jumped, not expecting anyone to be around, but Peter was behind him, moving Grey's hands out of the way.

No way could he mistake the wonderful smell of his mate. So outdoorsy and pine scented, it reminded him of Peter's green eyes. Grey swallowed. He needed to get his libido under control because any moment — a groan stopped his thoughts. It was too late — his cock was hard and throbbing and his mate could smell his desire. Peter was too close and touching him. His body was in overdrive, wanting to mate and make Peter his for good. Peter rested his head on Grey's and breathed in deep. Grey could hear every move Peter made.

He didn't want this moment to end. If he made any move, he'd scare Peter away and they'd be back to square one. Grey had to take it slow, let Peter lead.

"I want you."

"Pete — I'm not stopping you."

Peter walked around to stand in front of him. Grey's mouth watered at the sight of Peter. Peter's cock was hard and outlined in his pants, right there — all Grey had to do was reach out and touch.

"It's just sex."

Grey closed his eyes. Fuck. How could he convince Peter it was more than that?

"For now." Grey moved so he could nuzzle Peter's crotch.

He wanted skin and they were wearing too many clothes. Grey wasn't going to fight, not right now. He was too close to having a taste of his mate. But he wasn't letting this go and wouldn't let Peter put him in the fuck buddy category.

The zipper was right in front of him — Grey took it in his teeth and eased it down. Peter's fat heavy cock was there, ready to be tasted. He'd gone commando. That was so sexy Grey almost came right there. He had no control over his body.

"Suck me, Grey."

"What changed?" Grey had to know what had brought about this new attitude. This whole time Pete had been so standoffish — now he was giving in to his baser needs?

Pete looked confused. "Huh?"

Grey moved away, sitting back in his chair and not touching Pete.

"You're fighting me all the time. Why now? What changed?"

"Can't we just—"

"Have sex, because that's all we're good for?"

"No — that isn't — not — "

"So you're saying you want to try this — you and me? More than a quick fuck in the plane and then you go back to ignoring me or bitching at me?"

God, he was stupid. Pete was going to have sex with him and here he was questioning things. Why couldn't he just take what he could?

Because I want more. I deserve more.

Pete crossed his arms over his chest. This was the man that Grey knew. The one with a chip on his shoulder who was angry at the world. This Pete he could deal with.

"I'm horny and you can't deny you are too."

"So I'm just here to scratch an itch? You can do better than that."

"Screw you."

"No, thanks. Don't we have some pack members to find?"

"Fine. Breakfast is in the galley. I'll meet you outside."

Pete stalked off the plane, not even waiting for Grey to respond. He had no idea why he'd pushed it. Pete had finally shown a sexual interest in him and Grey should have run with it, consequences be damned. But he didn't know how to deal with Pete. He was such a stubborn wolf and Grey wanted to get his hands on whoever had fucked up his mate's life. Hell, Grey hadn't had it easy in his den, but no way would he let someone dictate his love life, he'd love the person he wanted to. Let them try and he'd beat them down. It was different with Pete. Sometimes he looked so sad, like he wanted more. Grey wanted to give it to him.

Not now. Not here. Grey didn't have time to seduce Pete to his way of thinking. They had to find the missing pack members and head home. Grey had more to worry about than his mate. His sister was out there somewhere, missing, maybe alone. They needed to get back to America and normalcy.

Grey went to find some food so they could get this crap over with.

* * * *

Who the hell did Greycen think he was? So what if Pete wanted a quick fuck? Was it his fault that, just once, he wanted to know what it would be like to have sex? To feel someone's arms wrapped around him in love. God, he wanted that so bad, but he was worthless. Grey had just confirmed it. Pete wasn't good enough even for a pity fuck. And now he was being stupid. Pete stormed down the plane steps. Maybe he'd take his cousin Everett on a road trip. Just them and their bikes with no one around for miles. At least until Grey left for his den, then he could return to his home. Pete gulped and rubbed his chest. It hurt to think of Grey leaving, but it was for the best. He was too tempting. Look what had almost happened. He'd walked into the cabin and seen Grey rubbing his neck and Pete had had to touch — the urge had been strong and before he'd known it he'd been behind Grey, massaging his back, working out the kinks. And those words had slipped out.

I want you.

But it was more than that. Pete craved Grey with a passion he hadn't known existed. It hurt to deny him, but he had to. They were abominations and he couldn't taint Grey or they'd both die. Hunted and shot down for wanting another man. His parents had told him they'd find him wherever he was if he so much as attempted to be with another guy. Pete believed them. There'd been a time a couple of years ago when Everett had dragged him to a gay bar. All he'd done was dance with a guy and his dad had been there with a knife. Cut him up real bad. He'd be dead if not for his cousin.

Nope, he wasn't bringing Grey into his life. It would be better if he left.

For who?

Pete closed his eyes and sat on the ground. The thoughts he was having were dangerous.

Your family can't find you here, dipshit. Do something. Fuck Grey. Let him fuck you. No one would know.

But he would know and the minute he stepped foot back in America his parents would show up. Probably kill him and Grey. No way in hell was that happening. It was safer this way. And he'd keep thinking that until he convinced himself.

Grey brushed past him and dropped a pack beside him.

"Do you have the coordinates Bella gave you for the necklace?"

"Yep. GPS too," Pete nodded.

"Great. The pilot is staying here with the plane. Let's get this over with."

There were no words between them as they made their way through the jungle. Grey was angry and Pete didn't blame him. The situation was fucked up and they really didn't have time to get into it. Pete had to get away from temptation and the damn pack had forced him into a situation that made it hard for him to keep his hands to himself.

Why do I have to?

Wasn't Grey some kind of protector? He could hold his own. All Pete had to do was explain the situation.

And there he went, thinking dangerous thoughts again.

They stopped for a water break. Everything looked the same. Pete looked down at the GPS. They had to be close.

"If we don't find it in a few hours we'll set up camp. I don't want to go tramping around in the dark in an unknown place. We'll take turns with the watch." That was the most Grey had said to him all day.

"Are you sure we can't push it a little more?"

"I don't know about you—but I'd like to get home alive. We don't know what kind of predators are out there or if there is some kind of ambush waiting. I want to be alert and ready for anything."

There wasn't anything Pete could say to that. Grey was right. Their break over, they continued their trek until they reached a clearing.

"Why haven't we seen the wreckage from the other plane?" Peter inquired.

"Good question. I have no idea, but what does this look like to you?" Grey waved him over.

Pete looked around—it was an odd place to be so open. He crouched down beside Grey.

"Is that... Hell it is—the necklace." Pete looked over at Grey.

Grey reached for it.

"Wait—" But Pete wasn't in time. The second Grey had the necklace in his grasp, he was flung back.

Pete rushed over. Grey didn't look hurt. He sat up and looked around.

"Fuck!"

"What happened?" Pete demanded.

"Joy spelled the damn thing. Now my head is pounding. I saw it. Everything. Ive and Djimon were captured by some native. Joy and Zareb went to destroy the Vessel." Grey tossed the necklace to the ground, like he couldn't get away from it fast enough.

"Did you see which way Ive was taken?" Pete kicked at it, but was careful not to actually touch it.

Grey pointed off to the right. Pete could make out a trail — barely, but it was there.

"I want to camp here tonight. When daylight hits we're going after Ive." Grey stood and brushed off his pants. His ass looked good enough to squeeze — but Pete wasn't going there.

He cleared his throat. "Not half-cocked. We can't race in there and save the day."

Grey gave him a look that said 'duh'. Pete just grinned back until he realised what he was doing and he looked down. He couldn't get chummy, it was too dangerous.

"We'll observe first, assess the situation and then take action. You ready for this?"

Fighting might be the only thing Pete was ready for. That was easy — emotions on the other hand could go fuck themselves.

"I'm ready. Let's start unpacking." Pete turned his back on Grey and rifled through his pack. There was a small pup tent inside and a few things to make a fire. He tossed them out and set up camp.

This was the life — roughing it outdoors under the night sky. He looked up and was amazed by all the stars. He really shouldn't have been, because the pack house was just as lovely at night — but this was different. He was a world away from his problems. Now, if he could just take what he really wanted. He shot a glance over at Grey to see him doing the same thing — setting up a tent a few feet away.

Would he have the balls to suggest they use one tent for body heat? Probably not. He'd freeze his balls off before getting that close to temptation again.

"You doing okay? How's the head?"

"Fine. I'll get the fire, you do dinner?" Grey wouldn't even look at him.

Good. That's what he wanted—wasn't it?

Pete rummaged through the bag for the MREs they'd packed. He didn't know where Russ came up with military rations, but he wasn't going to question it. They would do for tonight. If they were here much longer he'd go hunting to find some fresh meat.

He watched Grey through lowered lids, trying not to be too obvious. He knew it was ruined when his cock hardened. Warring scents were in the air. This tension had to be broken and he'd do it if he had to. Enough was enough. They might not be mates, but that didn't mean he couldn't have more. Screw his family.

Now he had to figure out how to talk to Grey about it without pissing him off. Did he even have to talk? He set the meals off to the side. Grey was looking at him now. Pete sat down and unzipped his pants. He was so hard it might not take much to get him off. Especially not with Grey watching him.

It was if the surrounding area faded away and it was only the two of them. Pete licked his lips, his breathing erratic. He wanted this so bad he could taste it. Not wanting to rush it and liking Grey's eyes on him he started off slow, stroking up and down. He paused to wipe the head of his cock, his pre-cum beading up. He rubbed it on his lips and sucked his thumb into his mouth. That was all it took to break Grey's control. Pete didn't think it would take much. Not with the way they wanted each other.

Grey kissed him and he moaned, tasting himself and Grey. Pete let go of his dick and wrapped his arms around Grey, bringing him closer. He didn't want either of them to think. Nothing here could break this moment. It was going to happen.

Chapter Four

Grey couldn't believe he was kissing Pete. One minute he was tending to the fire ignoring Pete and the next he was watching him jack off. The moment Pete touched his lips with his cum, Grey was a goner. He wanted to taste and he was going to.

All his plans to make Pete wait went out of the window. He was claiming his mate. Right here and right now. He almost lost it when Pete surrounded him with his arms. Pete was rocking against him and it couldn't be comfortable with his dick rubbing against his zipper. They should get undressed, but Grey was afraid of ruining the connection they had. If he moved the wrong way or said the wrong thing — this would end and he'd be back to having a surly mate.

Maybe if they shared this now, Pete would realise that they were meant for each other. Grey pressed Pete's body as close to his as he could get. It was starting to chill and would be best if they got into one of the tents.

He didn't bother suggesting it. He moved away from Pete and held out his hand. The true test was if Pete took it and followed him. Grey held his breath, hoping against hope that Pete would take it. His knees almost buckled as Pete took what was offered.

They stumbled into the tent, each rushing to get their clothes off. Pete finished first and looked so sexy sprawled out. The best thing was how intent Pete's stare was. Grey finally ditched the last of his clothes and crawled over to Pete. The tent was small and barely contained him. Pete's legs were hanging out of the front. He loved how tall he was and he wanted to taste every inch of him. Grey backed out of the tent, his bare ass cold, but he didn't care. He started with Pete's toes, sucking each digit. Pete squirmed, but didn't stop him. The noise he was making was driving Grey crazy. He refused to touch his own cock because he was afraid he'd come right then and there and that might wake Pete out of whatever had caused him to want this here and now.

Grey peppered kisses along Pete's long legs and nibbled at his inner thigh. Not wanting it to end too fast he only kissed the tip of Pete's cock before continuing up the lovely body. This was his mate, the man he'd spend forever with, and he wanted their first time to be the best. Who cared if they were in the middle of the jungle in a tent, it would be a moment to remember.

They were soon lost in each other's arms. The time and place didn't matter anymore. Grey had never known sex could be so—right. Pete filled his very being and made him whole and Grey hadn't even known he was broken. He buried his face in Pete's neck. Not the best idea because the urge to bite was strong. To bond them as one. Pete smelt of forest and home. Grey's teeth ached to pierce the skin, his mouth full of saliva. He wasn't going to be able to control himself. He was so far gone and one bite wouldn't bind them as mates. They needed the ritual and the words for Pete and he just won't release the mating serum. Grey gave in to the urge and sank his teeth in. Pete howled and threw his head back.

Pete returned the bite, sinking his teeth into Grey's neck, and they were both goners. He could feel Grey's hot release inside him. He exploded between them and a white light surrounded them as the ground shook. Grey thought it was because of the best orgasm he'd ever had and collapsed against Pete. That's when he felt it. A heat coursed through his body and Pete was there. It was the oddest sensation. He could feel what Pete was feeling. His mate was now a part of him.

How was that even possible?

Pete lay back down and Grey didn't want to move. The ground wasn't shaking anymore and he was tired. Grey was also afraid of how Pete was going to react. They were well and truly mates now. He just hoped Pete wouldn't think he'd tricked him, because he hadn't. This wasn't how mating was supposed to go. At least not from what he'd been told.

Neither of them said a word. Grey's breathing finally evened out and he wondered if he should say something. The growl of his stomach interrupted his thoughts and Pete laughed. It was musical and Grey wanted to hear more of it. He vowed to do what he could to make Pete happy.

"Weren't you getting dinner?" Grey rose up, using his arms to brace himself, and looked down at Pete.

"I was—distracted."

"I think you *were* the distraction." Grey pressed his lips to Pete's.

He had no plans on taking it further, but Pete had other ideas. He opened his mouth and ran his tongue along the crease of Grey's lips before flipping them over. Now Grey was under Pete and getting hard again.

Grey hadn't expected this playful Pete. He figured his mate would storm off, not kiss him again. He was happy and, if his mate sense was right, so was Pete. He didn't want it to change. He clutched Pete tight, wishing for time to stand still.

It was the strangest thing Pete had ever felt. He was happy. He hadn't felt this good in a really long time. The last time was when he'd gone with his cousin Everett on a cross-country motorcycle ride. He didn't want to stop kissing Grey and he was getting hard again. He wondered what it would feel like to have Grey inside him. Grey seemed to like it when Pete's cock was up his ass. Pete hadn't even had time to be nervous.

If he let himself really think about it, this was what he'd always wanted. Someone to call his own. But it still wasn't the case. They could never be—mates.

Oh, shit.

Pete pushed himself away from Grey. That light and these feelings…they weren't all his. It was as if a part of him now belonged to Grey. The happiness he felt wasn't all his. Why didn't he sense it sooner?

What had Grey done to him? His parents would kill them both for sure now. It didn't matter if they were a continent away. They would know that the abomination had mated. Russ couldn't even save him now. Pete stumbled out of the tent.

"Pete? What is it? You look like you've seen a ghost?" Grey followed him out.

Pete held out a hand to hold Grey off.

"Don't—please. We're both dead now. Don't you know what we've done? We can't have mates, it's forbidden and now they'll kill us." Pete was speaking fast and backing away. He stumbled on something and fell to the ground.

Grey rushed over to him, but Pete kept moving. Maybe if they didn't touch anymore no one would know.

"Pete—you're going to hurt yourself. Calm down and talk to me." Grey didn't get much closer and crouched down beside him.

"We can't be together. What did you do? If it was just sex they might never know—but we fuckin' *mated*. How is that possible? I thought there was—more." Pete took a deep breath and looked straight into Grey's blue eyes. "My family is going to kill us. That's a fact. I'm an abomination and now I've made you dirty, too." Pete looked down at the ground.

He sounded so weak, but it couldn't be helped. He'd just signed Grey's death sentence.

"I don't know who told you that bullshit, but you're a beautiful man and you're perfect. No one is going to kill us. Russ isn't like that. At least I didn't get that from him when—"

"Stop. Just stop. I'm not talking about the pack. I'm talking about my *family*—the ones who kicked me out. They always show up. I was warned." Pete looked around like they might appear here, in Africa. He knew that was silly, but he was totally freaked out.

"Babe—I won't let those bastards touch you," Grey growled and gathered him close.

Pete let him for a second. Grey made him safe, but it was an illusion, one he couldn't get used to. He took this one minute for himself and let Grey comfort him. The anger he felt surge through him wasn't his own. It was odd having these sensations. Maybe, for tonight, he could forget and tomorrow he could go back to the way things were. He wanted the safety Grey gave him. One night. That's all he asked. Then he'd find a way to protect Grey from his family. They wouldn't hurt his…mate. God, Grey really was his mate. What did this mean? Nothing good could come of this, Pete was sure.

"Let me get us something to eat. We should probably—ah—dress, first." Pete looked down at himself. He was dirty from his crawl across the ground.

He stood and dusted himself off before putting his pants back on. Grey didn't say anything and Pete could feel his confusion. Pete didn't blame him. He had no idea what to do right now.

The MREs were still on the ground where he'd dropped them. Pete opened them up and cooked what needed cooking. Nothing too fancy, they never were. He handed one to Grey and sat down beside him.

Grey didn't eat. He kept looking at Pete and it was making him nervous, but he didn't move away. There would be time for that tomorrow. The food wasn't that good, but it was enough to appease his hunger. He took Grey's trash from him and put it in a bag he'd set aside for disposables. He didn't want to litter, the place was too beautiful and primitive.

This time he held out his hand for Grey, not sure if it would be accepted. Neither spoke as Pete guided them into the tent. It would be a tight fit with both of them in there, but he didn't care. He would make the most of his one night. They both kept their pants on—Pete would have liked to have Grey inside him, but one mark was enough. For now he would hold Grey. He zipped the tent and turned to see Grey underneath the sleeping bag he'd spread out. He'd have to curl up to fit inside the tent. Grey let him get settled before pulling him close and throwing a leg over Pete and cuddling him close.

Pete had never experienced this kind of tender love. Not that he could remember, anyway. Once he'd realised he was gay, it was like his parents knew and kept him at a distance. They'd tried to ignore it when he'd come out, but then the beating had happened and he'd been banished from his tribe.

He didn't want to think about the things he'd had to do to survive before he'd found his cousin Ev. Everett had been the only bright spot in his life—until now. And this was just a passing phase. But he wouldn't think on that. Not now when Grey was curled around him and softly snoring. He'd live in this moment and store the memory to keep forever, even if he couldn't keep Grey beyond tonight.

Chapter Five

Ive licked Dji's chest. He was naked and all hers for the taking. God, he was beautiful—his skin so dark against hers. She loved running her fingers over his body—the way he shivered for her made her wet. Tasting every inch of him seemed like a great idea. Ive worked her way down his body taking tiny nibbles on her way to his glorious cock. Her ultimate goal was to swallow him down. Maybe she'd let him come, maybe she wouldn't.

She'd play it by ear and enjoy every second of it. Her hair trailed over his body until he grabbed it in his fist, holding it out of her way, but not stopping her.

A small tug had her looking up. Dji grinned at her. She winked back before taking the head of his cock in her mouth. He closed his eyes and threw his head back. Ive was happy she'd been watching him. His hips bucked up, but she held him down. Ive wasn't ready to take him deep yet. First she wanted to pay special attention to his slit, wiggling her tongue back and forth—his flavour was salty with a hint of sweet.

She could easily become addicted to the way he tasted.

Dji moaned. She did that to him, made him lose control. It was a heady feeling. She closed her eyes and hummed as she slid down, taking him to the root, her nose buried in his curly hair. What would he feel like inside her? Ive squirmed, but couldn't get the friction she needed. Dji shifted and she straddled his leg—it still wasn't enough, but she didn't want to stop sucking him.

He took the decision away from her, tugging at her hair.

"Ive—gonna—please—stop. Want inside... God, woman—too much—please..."

His hips jerked and she had to move back or gag. She moved back up his body. Her lips hovered over his—wait—was that? Did she smell—smoke? She tried to look around, but Ive didn't want to open her eyes. Were they at the crash site? Why would they be having sex there? Where were the others? It didn't make sense. Her face hurt, but she didn't remember being injured in the crash. She remembered it all too well, they'd been kidnapped. She opened her eyes to see that she was tied to a post and Dji was beside her, also trussed up. This couldn't be good. Ive looked around. There wasn't much to the tribe. Dji was slumped until something made him stand up tall.

A native walked up to Dji and smacked him in the face with the butt of his spear.

The action, out of the blue startled her and Ive screamed.

"What are you doing? Stop!" She knew they wouldn't stop just because she was upset, but at this point she didn't care.

Why were they hurting him? Dji had done nothing. Like there was anyone around for them to speak to. And Dji had barely said a word since he was released from Dmitri.

"Who you talk to?"

The guy spoke English, that had to be good, but were they crazy? Dji hadn't spoken to anyone and he remained silent now. The tribesman walked off, leaving them alone as if he were following someone.

"Dji, talk to me — please. What's going on?"

"We can't talk right now, they won't allow it."

And he was right. If they saw them they could get hit again and she didn't want to chance that. Dji's face had to be on fire. She knew hers was from that damn slap. She wished they'd had time to bind, but nothing on this trip had gone right. Dji was still not in his full power and in a cloud of guilt she could almost feel it. They needed to stay as far under the radar as they could. Joy and Zareb would come looking for them. It was only a matter of time. She just didn't know if it would be before or after they destroyed the damn Vessel.

Don't jump, don't react. It's me — Djimon.

How — Ive looked over at Dji, pushing her thoughts at him.

She didn't think this was possible for an unmated pair.

Don't look at me or they'll know. They might figure it out. I don't know if I can shield myself from the shaman for long. Joy's spirit was here. It's a trap and I warned her. They will destroy the Vessel first and come for us unless I can get us out of here first. I'm still not at full strength.

Ive faced forward. This was the most Dji had spoken to her since he'd come into himself. She would do what she must to make sure they survived. How, she

41

had no idea. It was at times like this she wished she had magical abilities. For now, she worked on her ropes. Her shoulders were hurting from the position she was in and she needed to pee. Not the best situation, but maybe she could get them free after they let her go to the bathroom. But Dji was right—he wasn't at his full power and still in a funk. Until he got out of that he'd be useless. There was only so much she could do alone and she didn't know how far out Joy and Zareb were.

I'll be ready.

Ive wanted to reassure Dji and hoped she could keep her promise. One of the tribesmen came closer and pointed at her. She had no idea what he was going on about but he untied her and dragged her to a secluded section. She looked back at Dji. He struggled with his bonds and growled. Ive didn't like it any more than he did, but she didn't have a choice in the matter.

She was pushed into an area with a hole dug out. The tribesman pointed to her, then to the hole. Ive was confused for a moment until it hit her. This was her potty break. She didn't have time for modesty. She had to go and the guy wasn't turning around. Not that she could speak to him anyway. She had no idea who spoke English and who didn't.

Once she was done she was tied back up. Dji looked her over. At least his protective instincts were alive and well. She hoped they all made it out alive. She was beginning to have her doubts. Water was shoved into her face and it was either drink or drown. At least they weren't torturing them.

That could be bad. It might mean they were going to use them for something else. They wanted the Vessel and who knew how many spirits were trapped inside.

If they tried to possess Dji again, it could break him for good. What was she going to do?

The shaman came back to her. Dji looked out of it again. She didn't know if it was an act or if he was really so far into himself he wouldn't be able to help. Ive wanted to shake him and make him realise that it was going to get better.

"Tell me now — where is the Vessel? I will go easy on you."

Ive didn't say anything.

"No worries. I think I know — I hope you are ready to sleep for a while. Once we have the Vessel, you too will be turned. I wonder what delightful spirits are left in there." The shaman laughed and left her to her own thoughts. It was getting dark and she was tired. Not that she could sleep in this position. She wasn't naïve enough to think that they would untie them so they could go to bed — yeah, right, bed. More like standing up and not even a sleeping bag in sight.

She would need what strength she could get. Ive meditated and took herself to a happier place. Letting her body get the rest it would need. Hopefully she wouldn't have long to wait for the big rescue. At least she knew Joy and Zareb were alive to help them out. Now she had to sit and wait. Something she'd never been good at. Maybe she could go back to her dream and finish what she'd started. If she couldn't have the actual Dji yet, her dream self could enjoy.

* * * *

Light was coming over the horizon, daylight was upon them and Dji knew he'd need to be prepared. He had people to protect and it was about time he did something other than kill people.

He would never be able to forget what Dmitri had done while in possession of his body. Dji had much to atone for, but right now he had to get his mate out of this situation before the shaman did something stupid. All he could do now was gather what strength he could, so he was ready when the others arrived.

It was the first time in a long time he felt useful. He kept to himself, not expending his energy. Dji would be ready.

He dozed off and on and saw the unbelievable. His brother Baakir was leading Zareb and Joy into the tribe. It looked like they were bound together and the two were led to the poles where he and Ive were tied. This couldn't be good. How were they caught in the trap? He'd warned Joy this would happen. It couldn't end like this. Anger welled inside him. He didn't want to be a puppet any longer.

"I'm going to untie you. Can you stand?" Zareb spoke, but his lips didn't move.

Dji gave a slight nod that he understood. Zareb worked at the ropes on his hands and soon he was free.

"Joy said that two others from the Masters' tribe are here somewhere. Be on the lookout for them. Kir is with us."

"Not possible."

"It is. How do you think I ended up unbound and able to untie you? We've spoken and he is coming back with us. Be prepared because things might go a little crazy in a minute."

The shaman walked up to them looking entirely too pleased with himself. Kir wasn't far behind. The shaman spared a glance for Ive and Joy and it seemed as if they were to be untied as well. Things were looking up, but how were they going to escape this mess?

It was his fault. If he'd been more with it after the plane crash he could have prevented their capture.

"What have we here? Kir says he has the Vessel. If that is the case I no longer need any of you—not your souls anyway. Djimon, I'm sure Dmitri is ready to come home now. What do you think?" the shaman taunted.

That was the last straw. The energy burned hot inside him. Dji rose up and up, his feet no longer on the ground, and he snarled. He held his hand in front of him and released lightning into the shaman. He would *not* allow his body to be possessed again. He was stronger than that now and had a few of Dmitri's tricks up his sleeve. His soul hadn't always been dormant when Dmitri was in control. He supposed he could thank the spirit for that at least.

Ive came towards him and so did Zareb. One stood on each side of him. They spoke to him, but he didn't hear. He released more lightning, rocking the camp with explosions. He wasn't even aiming anymore.

It finally sunk in that everyone was safe and it was time for him to stop. Zareb and Ive had got through to him. The shaman was destroyed, as was half of the tribe.

"We're fine. Zareb said the Vessel has been destroyed. It's over. You're done now, right?" Ive was stroking his arm. It was soothing in a way nothing had been in a very long time.

Dji dropped to the ground and sobs racked his body. It was a release that he'd needed for a very long time. The possession and the atrocities Dmitri had committed while in his body. The loss of control and the guilt that never seemed to go away. It pressed in tight and the only way to let go was through tears. He'd killed again. He was a monster and deserved to be put down.

He vaguely heard Ive tell Joy the situation was under control as she tried to comfort him. Zareb was still there, too, and he calmed down. He wasn't going back. There was more talk about the camp, but Dji closed his eyes and focused on getting himself completely under control. The power surge was draining. He didn't notice when Ive left, but Zareb didn't leave his side.

"We're going to take you to the place where we buried the Vessel so you can see for yourself that the evil is so far under no one can get to it. I think it'll help you feel whole again, brother. And it's going to be better, Dji, once we get back to America. I promise you."

Some of the fog he'd been under was lifting. He didn't fully believe that things would magically be okay once they left Africa, but it might be a start. When he got back he'd have to decide what he wanted to do. It might be best if he left and sequestered himself from people. Maybe he'd live fully as his cat, but he wasn't making any decisions while he wasn't yet fully functional.

He began to pace the camp and wondered when they could start moving to the place where the Vessel was buried. They should go now. There was no need to wait. Ive came out of the bush looking fresh and a bit happy. She walked right up to him.

"It'll be fine, my mate. Let me help and things will be okay."

She smelt heavenly and he must smell horrid.

"We're going to bathe. I think we'll all feel better." Zareb gestured for Dji to follow him.

Not really having much choice, he went. If he'd known where the site was he'd have started off there and then. He might stink, but it was better to have the evil in a place no one would find it again.

The women had left the soap on a rock by the edge of the water. Dji didn't spend much time bathing, his mind on other things. Like how it would feel to finally be completely free and live his life. He remembered a time when he'd been happy. He'd been ready to be a protector of his tribe and do the right thing. The song from the Vessel had been too strong and he'd opened it only to lose his life. There was no other way to explain being awake and not able to control your body. To go against everything he'd ever been taught. He'd tried time and again to wrestle control away, but Dmitri had always been too strong. It had taken another shifter's mate to bring him back to the world of the living. Something he'd never have been able to do for himself.

Zareb brought him out of his thoughts by tapping his shoulder. It was then that Dji noticed the other two men in the water with them. He wondered who they were, but didn't have time to question them. It was time to be done with the Vessel.

They made a formation with his brother, Kir taking the lead. The two unknowns were in front of him, with Zareb and Joy taking the rear position.

"Ive — who are those two men?" There was time now that the trek had begun.

"The small redhead is my twin, Greycen, and the other is his mate, Peter."

"Two men?"

"Yes, that isn't a problem, is it?"

Ive bristled. Dji didn't think he'd ever seen that before. His mate was usually so calm and in charge.

"No. I've just never seen it before."

He really didn't care. It was an oddity to him, nothing more. Fate put mates together and, if the Ancients decreed it so, who was he to make judgement? He was weak and he stumbled. Ive came closer to support him. The power he'd used was a little too much for the state he'd been in. He hated feeling weak.

The man Ive had said was her brother fell back to help, supporting his other side. He could see the resemblance now. Peter, Greycen's mate, kept looking back to check on them. He hoped he could have that with Ive, but he was beginning to think that having a mate was lost to him. He had too much to do to redeem himself.

Chapter Six

Grey was ready for this nightmare of a mission to be over. They were all tired and Pete wasn't talking to him, again. After they'd woken up, they'd headed in the direction the necklace had indicated. Pete was as surly as ever, like the night before hadn't happened. It broke Grey's heart. It was as if they'd taken one step forward, then two back. He was beginning to think he would have to go home to his den. He didn't want to live with the other foxes. He wanted to stay with the wolves and his mate, but seeing Pete day in and day out without being able to touch him would kill him.

He'd caught Pete looking back at him a few times as if checking on him, but, every time Grey had managed to catch his gaze, Pete would turn back around. Grey couldn't take it anymore. For now he'd let it drop. He wasn't the type to give in easily, but Pete wore him down. They'd worked well together when they'd reached the camp. Then Dji had gone crazy and all hell had broken loose. They hadn't even been needed so it was a waste of effort on their part. If they'd had more time to work as a team—maybe Pete would be walking beside him, not in front of him.

The only thing they were good for was a ride home. And would he even be going home? He wanted to talk to his sister, but she'd been so preoccupied with her mate she hadn't even had time to say 'hi'. He was just relieved to see her alive.

"How're you doing, Ive?"

"I'm good as I can be, Grey. Thank you for coming."

"I wouldn't be anywhere else. Had to pull your butt out of the fire—again." Grey managed a small smile.

"This is true."

Dji moaned between them and stumbled again. He was too weak. That was the only reason the group had forgone shifting to make the journey quicker. Grey hoped it wasn't much longer. The big guy was heavy, even with Ive supporting some of his weight.

"You weren't hurt too bad, were you?" He was worried about his sister, but knew not to baby her. She was a strong protector and he was proud of her.

"It'll take more than a slap or two to bring me down, but I think I should ask how bad you're hurt." Ive gave him 'the look'. The one that said she thought she knew more than she did. He'd hated seeing that growing up.

"I'll be fine." Grey spared a glance ahead to see Pete looking back. He gave him a wink and was surprised. Pete actually smiled back at him before the frown returned.

"Sure you will. You're mated, aren't you? Yet he still keeps his distance?"

"And you aren't mated—what's up with that?" He wanted to shift the conversation away from him.

By now, after their night together he and Pete had, the two of them should be in a better place.

"We have a few issues to get through before Dji and I can get to that." Ive rolled her eyes.

"I'm sorry, my mate." Dji injected.

Grey hadn't realised he was fully conscious. Ive must not have noticed either because she jerked just a little. If someone didn't know her, they wouldn't have seen it. She was quick to put her ice mask back in place. The one she showed the world to hide her emotions. Something he'd never developed.

"No need to apologise. We'll get to that technicality when we get to America and the Master's compound." Ive assured Dji and the other shifter went back to his almost catatonic state.

"That's another thing—we shouldn't have bonded. Pete and I. We didn't do the ritual."

He didn't know what was worse—feeling Pete's emotions or never knowing they existed. For all his standoffishness, Pete yearned for him, so now he not only felt his own ache, but Pete's too. Sometimes life sucked.

Dji spoke up again, "It's the magic of our native land. When you're here, you don't need the words, just a bite between soulmates and you are joined—well, and the sex. If you have those two things—the mating is complete."

Grey was going to have to watch what he said—obviously Dji was paying more attention than he let on. But that was good to know. Fate hadn't only given him a mate who didn't believe he deserved one, but it had also fucked him over by mating them before Pete was ready. Behind that ache, Pete was freaking out something awful. Grey wanted to know more about Pete's family. They'd royally screwed him over and, if Grey had his way, he'd kill them all for making his fearless mate doubt himself.

"We are here," Kir announced.

Grey stopped and let go of his sister's mate. Their talk had made the trek pass faster than he had expected. It was almost time to leave and he couldn't wait to see that plane, even though it meant another long flight. When he got to the Masters' pack house he'd sleep for a day—if Pete let him. Hopefully together, in a nice big bed they'd both fit in. A guy could dream.

* * * *

"I think it best if Dji, Kir and I enter the circle together. The rest of you wait here. We'll only be a moment. Then we can head for the plane." Zareb came to take Ive's place at Dji's side, Kir on the other, both supporting him.

They stopped and allowed Dji to sit right on top of the spot where Joy and Zareb had buried the Vessel. It was stronger than he'd expected it to be.

"I can feel the evil," Dji said in a defeated tone.

He was tired of being the Vessel's bitch. Dmitri's soul was trapped below the Earth in a sealed container. He should've been elated, but he could still feel the anger and hatred below.

"You may feel it, but it is contained. I think the only reason you sense it is because it was a part of you for so long. Even now, the vibrations are weaker than they were when Joy and I buried it. The magic we used was strong." Zareb tried to reassure him.

"Someone will have to come back and check on this spot from time to time to make sure. No one should have to live through what I did." That was something Dji would insist on.

Being trapped in your own body wasn't something he'd wish on his worst enemy.

"I agree. I will talk with Russ when we return. I think we all could use some downtime. Kir should settle in and you need time to adjust."

"I need to—" Dji bowed his head and placed his hands on the ground. He began to chant, using some of his own magic to help seal the spot. It flowed through him.

It was almost too much for his body in its weakened state, but it had to be done. He slumped over, but righted himself. Not needing any help, he stood. For the first time in weeks, Dji began to have some hope.

"It should have been me," Zareb whispered.

"No, my brother. It was as it was meant to be." And, in his heart, he knew that it was his destiny. It was horrible, but true.

"You were the serious one—the man whom the tribe looked up to. I was the joker, the one who tempted you into all the trouble."

Dji put a hand on Zareb's shoulder to offer a little comfort.

"Do you not see? That's why we were perfect to be guardians together. It was a balance."

"How can you forgive me?" Zareb looked more dejected than Dji had ever remembered seeing him. He was not the same carefree man from Dji's past.

"It wasn't your fault and you need to forgive yourself. Our paths are once again in line."

"I see you are feeling more like yourself. It is good to have you back." Zareb hugged Dji close.

"We should go now. I'm sure the others are getting impatient to leave," Kir broke in.

"It's good to be back. I'm ready to get to know who I am again and it seems, along the way, I have acquired a mate." The fog was all but gone.

He was a bit tired, but this was the him he remembered. The guilt still hovered on the edge of his consciousness, but he put it on the back burner.

Zareb threw back his head and laughed.

"Yes, you have, as have I. Now we have to get Kir squared away and life will be good."

"That is not nice. I am fine without a mate. I am just happy the evil is buried and gone. Too long have we wallowed in misery." Kir slapped him on the back.

The three left the clearing and went to join the others. It was almost as if they were in the past again. Brothers in spirit, if not blood. The newness washed over him when they reached the others and he finally got a good look at his mate. She was beautiful. She had long red hair and creamy white skin with the deepest blue eyes he'd ever seen. She was taller than most, and strong. She deserved better than him.

They walked to the plane in the same order as they'd come to the circle. Dji was a little rejuvenated and he was able to walk on his own.

"Ive, are you originally from the Master's pack?"

They knew so little of each other. Maybe they could chat. Not that it mattered, they were fated to be together. All they had to do was complete the bond. Ive smelt wonderful, like freshly cut grass on a spring day. He was becoming aroused for the first time in a long time. His mind screamed mate, and his body wanted to act on it.

"No. I'm a fox shifter. I was a protector to the princess of our den and a vision led us both to the Masters pack. Her mate is the alpha, Russ. I knew I had to help you. You needed me and I was there." Ive shrugged.

Just like that, she'd given up her life to search for him and he'd been an empty shell until now. Things could have gone so differently.

"The fog is just lifting—things have been unclear for such a long time."

"That's why I'm here, to help. I am your other half." Ive winked at him.

"I don't even know who I am anymore."

"We'll figure it out together. We have time. There's no rush." Ive squeezed his arm and they continued to walk. "What is the first thing you want to do when we reach the pack house?" Ive wanted to know.

"I—I've got no idea. I guess find out if I'm even welcome. I did a lot of bad things as Dmitri."

"But they know you weren't yourself. You and Dmitri were never the same person and you helped save Valerie when Dmitri kidnapped her. Do you think she would have escaped if you hadn't taken over your body? You're stronger than you give yourself credit for. You just didn't have the need to push Dmitri out."

She had so much confidence in him. More than he had in himself. They reached the plane before he was ready. He was enjoying talking to Ive and there was still so much to discover. They did have a long flight, but he was tired and needed a nap to help gain his strength. A good meal wouldn't hurt, either.

He wondered again how much of a welcome he would really receive. He didn't remember much of his time at the pack house after Dmitri was expelled from his body. His whole life had been one big fog. Now he needed to break out of it.

Could he redeem himself enough to take Ive as a mate or was he still too weak? When they got to the plane, Ive sat next to him and he only wanted to close his eyes for a second, but the last thing he remembered was Ive laying her head on his shoulder. Peace washed over him as he drifted off.

Chapter Seven

Pete sat as far from Grey as he could get. It was time to distance himself even further. It hurt, but he had to give up Grey forever. It was best for both of them, no matter how much his heart ached.

Grey would find someone new—he didn't even want to think about it. Once the flight was off and in the air, Pete went to the restroom. Anything to give him distance. He needed to splash some water on his face as well—if he fell asleep he might dream and that would make him crave Grey even more.

When he left the restroom, Zareb stopped him.

"Have a seat." Zareb gestured to the seat close to him.

"I was going to go back t—" he tried, but Zareb interrupted him.

"And you will, Peter, but we need to have a chat."

They both kept their voices low so they wouldn't wake the others, and Zareb wasn't going to take no for an answer.

"About what?" Pete was confused.

"Why you are not with your mate?" Zareb pointed to the front of the cabin where Grey rested.

Pete followed Zareb's finger and looked with longing on to his mate, wishing he could curl up beside him.

"I don't have a mate," Pete stated firmly.

He knew it was a lie, the bond tugged at him every second. Pete had no idea why fate was so cruel.

"Yes, Peter, you do," Zareb insisted. His anger was rising and that wasn't good. They needed to keep this between them.

"Gay men don't have mates." Pete crossed his arms over his chest, but he didn't make a move to leave.

"I do not know who told you that—as Joy would say—'bullshit', but it is false. The Ancients give us all mates. Some of us are lucky enough to find them in this lifetime. Do you know how long I've been alive? A very long time. I was born in the early sixteen hundreds and I had to wait for Joy. You had better believe I will not be letting her go any time soon. Think about this, young wolf. How will you feel when he finds another man to be with?"

Pete growled low in his throat. No way could Grey have another man. He might think it, but to have someone else say it out loud was too much.

"That is what I thought. Do not wait too long or he could leave. There is no guarantee he will stay with the Master's pack. He has a home to go to, the fox den. He doesn't need to guard Russ' mate anymore." Zareb patted Pete on the shoulder.

Pete nodded and left. He didn't rush, but went past the first seat he was in to sit in the same row with Grey. He shouldn't be doing this. It was too much to hope they could make something work.

There was noise from the back of the cabin. Pete noticed that Joy and Zareb were gone from their seats. He smiled at the first scream. The two must be mating. His cock got hard thinking of the others having sex. It reminded him that he still wanted to feel Grey inside him. He wanted to know what it would feel like to be fucked. He'd loved the way Grey's tight hole felt around his dick. He moaned without realising it.

He looked over at Grey to see if he'd heard, and Grey was awake. His blue eyes were serious. It was Pete's fault that Grey was so unsure. He was blowing hot and cold. He knew it, but Pete didn't know any other way. This was the first time he'd let himself even think it could be possible.

Could his family have been wrong? And why did he care what they thought after all these years? The threat was real, but they hadn't been around in a really long time. He had to stop living in fear. He took Grey's hand and kissed his palm before entwining their fingers. Just that little touch calmed him. He finally settled down and fell asleep, still holding Grey's hand.

* * * *

A bus picked them up at the airstrip. Pete had half expected Ev to be there, but he didn't see him anywhere. The trip to the pack house was short. Pete didn't say anything, just pulled Grey into the house, bypassing the others. They were talking, but there was something Pete wanted more. He wouldn't be included in whatever pack meeting Russ wanted to have the next day. He wasn't part of the core group and he was happy for it. They seemed to have the most troubles and the greatest power. Most days he was happy to just be a shifter with any sort of power.

Grey went along without a word. Pete was happy because he was afraid that, if Grey said anything, he might change his mind and he really didn't want to. He was just happy he had lube in his bedroom. Tonight he was going to lose his virginity completely. They reached his room and he opened the door.

It wasn't much to look at. Pete didn't need a lot of stuff. He had a bookcase full of books, a bed, a nightstand and a dresser. He finally felt like this was home and was settling in.

"Why now? You're confusing me here, Pete." Grey rubbed his forehead like he had a headache.

"I—damn it—I don't know. You make me want things I didn't know I wanted. Can we have tonight and talk tomorrow?"

"Depends. You gonna stop talking to me like last time?"

His face was hot, he knew he must be blushing. He'd acted like a jackass.

"No—we'll talk. I'll be honest, Grey, I don't know if we can do this, but right now I have this need to have you inside me. I ache for you. Please." Pete held out his hand.

Grey took it and led Pete to the bed. He was nervous and happy that Grey was taking charge.

"Lube?"

Pete pointed to his nightstand. He kept some stashed because it felt good when he masturbated. He never thought it would get to the point where he'd have someone to share his bed with. Tonight he would put the fear aside.

Grey pushed him on the bed, but this time—he wanted to taste. In the tent, Grey had kissed every inch of him and he'd fallen apart. He wanted to do that for Grey. Pete rolled them until he was on top. They stared at each other for a moment. Without looking away he took the lube from the drawer and tossed it on the bed. They'd need it later, but, for now, Pete had some tasting to do. He started with Grey's eyelids and kissed them closed before brushing his lips against Grey's. Pete didn't deepen the kiss, he had too much skin to taste.

"We have on too many clothes, Pete," Grey chuckled and thrust up.

Pete moaned. Grey was just as hard as he was. Pete ran his hands under Grey's shirt and inched it up his body. Grey tried to help, but Pete tangled his hands up and managed to cover Grey's eyes in the process. Pete kissed him then. Grey was all but helpless, but didn't struggle. He leaned into the kiss, opening his mouth so Pete could enter. He could kiss Grey for days.

The two hugged each other close and kissed some more. He really couldn't get enough of Grey's taste, but Grey was urging him for more.

"Want it to last. Please." Pete wasn't above begging.

He'd never had this before and they were connected in a way Pete had never experienced. In the end he couldn't slow it down forever. His first time was more than he'd ever expected it to be. Not that he should have been surprised. Grey wouldn't hurt him, at least not intentionally, and he wanted to do it again—but maybe later.

Pete crushed Grey to him and kissed him before they both collapsed on the bed. Grey fell on top of Pete and Pete didn't want to ever let go.

They finally calmed down enough for Pete to get a wash cloth. He was thankful he had his own bathroom. Grey was dozing when he got back. Pete washed him down and took the rag back to the bathroom, cleaning himself off.

He shut off all the lights and glanced out of the window. He jumped back. His worst nightmare was about to come true. Outside—his mother and father stood looking up to his room. It wasn't possible—how could they have got on to Masters' land? He had to be hallucinating. But what if he wasn't?

Pete backed away from the window and looked at the bed. He'd promised, but he couldn't stay there. What if they hurt Grey? Pete would never forgive himself. He grabbed some sweats and tiptoed out of the room. He'd go to the gym for a workout. He had to think.

Chapter Eight

Ive was exhausted and it looked like Dji was as well. They'd been given a guest suite. There was no question they'd spend the night together. If truth be told, she was a little nervous. She'd dreamt of this moment for such a long time and fate had claimed them to be mates.

Dji was better. She could feel it. It was odd because she shouldn't feel this connected to him without the mate bond, but she was. Once they'd left Africa, Dji had relaxed. She knew it had to do with the burial of the Vessel. She was happy it was out of their lives for good.

Tomorrow they had a meeting with Russ, but tonight was theirs, if they could get past being so tired.

"Dji—we can wait—"

"We could, but I want you, Ive. I haven't felt this strongly in a very long time. Every fibre of my being is saying it wants you. I don't know if it's the smart thing to do right now, but I don't care. I need you in my arms."

"Thank God." Ive walked over to Dji and stepped into his arms. She'd waited for this moment for a long time. This Dji she wanted to know more of. The guilt was still a part of him, but he was...whole. Before, he'd appeared dejected and...broken.

Ive looked into his eyes and ran her hands over his face, touching every inch. She used her thumbs to soothe the crinkle in his forehead and traced his nose before landing on his lips. He never blinked. Dji's eyes were so brown they were almost black. She could drown in them. His skin—so dark compared to her fair complexion.

Dji walked her back towards the bed, but stopped before she fell. Ive continued to look at him, but now she was taking off her clothes. They should probably shower. She looked over Dji's shoulders to see a bathroom.

"I want to wash the travel off me. Join me?" Ive finished removing her pants and shirt, leaving a trail behind her.

She didn't look back. She knew Dji would follow and she wasn't disappointed. Ive bent over to start the water. Dji caressed her back, paying close attention to her ass, squeezing the globes. Ive wished she could see his hands on her skin. The moan escaped her before she could even think to stop it.

It was wonderful having his hands on her and Dji being fully there for the first time. Ive had to focus to get the water to the right temperature before turning in his arms. He lifted her up and Ive wrapped her legs around his waist. He was rock hard—everywhere. Dji was as naked as she was—the first skin on skin contact was heaven, but paradise was his lips on hers. The first touch and she swore she saw sparks fly. The lights flickered and the bulb above the sink shattered.

"What the—" Ive mumbled against Dji's lips.

"Sorry—it's been a long time since I had—ah—this kind of contact and my control over my magic is rocky at best right now. We're lucky that's the only thing exploding or this would be over before it even started."

"Got it." Ive let go of Dji and entered the shower, holding the curtain open for him. It was a tight fit, but Ive wouldn't have had it any other way.

She wasn't scared of his power. It turned her on in ways she'd never imagined. He was so strong. Ive licked her lips in anticipation. Normally she liked to be in control, call it her protector instincts, but here—now, she wanted to give in to him and let him take over.

Dji pushed her against the shower tiles. They were cool against her back. Steam started to rise from the hot water. Ive spread her legs—Dji fit right in the cradle of her thighs, his cock hard against her belly. She couldn't wait to have his dick inside her, but for now she'd relish being surrounded by him in the heated cocoon of the shower.

Ive ran her hands down his body, lightly scratching him with her nails. He didn't stop her as she kneaded his ass and squeezed, but he did kiss her. Ive melted into that kiss and held on tighter. She was so excited her breath came out in pants. She had to calm down. Dji seemed to sense she needed a break. He nuzzled her jaw and reached for the soap. Lathering his hands up, he started at her shoulders and worked his way down. It was the best foreplay she'd ever experienced. Her body tingled with his every touch. The soapy hands were more erotic than she'd thought humanly possible and she trembled. His fingers glided over her body. The only sounds were the patter of the water against the shower curtain and their breathing as she gasped and moaned. Ive's pussy throbbed and she wanted Dji's cock inside her.

The smell was almost overpowering between her and Dji's mating scent. It was as if they were back in the jungle. Ive leaned her head against the wall and closed her eyes, letting her other senses take over. Dji's hands were squeezing her breasts and tweaking her nipples. He twisted hard, bringing her to her tiptoes.

"Oh, God," Ive moaned.

"Too much?" Dji didn't let up and continued to twist.

"No—more, please." It was delicious and oh so good. She could feel the pull in her pussy.

No one had ever been rough with her and she was finding she liked the different sensations. The gentle caress followed by the pinch of pain. What she wanted most right now was for him to slam her against the tiles and fuck her against the wall. There was so much to explore with this dominant man and she wanted every second of it. Other men she'd been with were weak in comparison, totally forgettable. She'd never forget Dji and never wanted to—she growled low in her throat just thinking about it. Dji let go of her nipples and she relaxed, the pain mixing with pleasure through every inch of her body. Ive was unprepared for the bite. He didn't break the skin, but he worried her tight bud between his teeth before soothing it with his tongue. He repeated it over and over, driving her nuts. It was even better than his fingers. She clutched at his shoulders—it was more intense than anything she'd ever felt. Ive thrust her hips, needing Dji inside her.

Ive's orgasm racked her body, but Dji didn't let her calm down, her body still throbbed. Coming from someone playing with her breasts had never happened before. There were so many firsts with her mate. His teeth scraped her stomach until he reached her pussy and buried his nose in her tight red curls. Dji knelt in front of her, she still had a tight hold on his shoulders. She needed it for balance. His tongue fucked her, mimicking what she wanted him to do with his cock. She was empty and only he could fill her. She spread her legs wider.

She didn't have a chance to come down because he ramped up every nerve of her body. He bit her pussy. Again, she was on her toes. She didn't know if she wanted to back away or lean into the feelings. Dji soothed her with kisses. Now, he was using his fingers, but it still wasn't enough. Her body was on fire. She'd be bruised tomorrow, but didn't care. She needed more. One finger became two, then three, faster and faster he thrust inside her. Dji slowed down and she whimpered, so turned on she was close to coming again—if she'd ever stopped from the first time. Each sensation rolled into the other.

"Ah! Oh, God, Dji—please, please—oh fuck—please..."

Dji stopped and Ive sobbed. She was so close—to what she didn't know, but it couldn't end now. He shut off the water and scooped her up into his arms.

"Dji, Dji, Dji—" she chanted his name.

He tossed her onto the bed and spread her legs wide. She helped him by grabbing her thighs and holding them up. She was so wet, not just from the shower, but from Dji's manipulation of her body. Ive didn't know what would happen next. She thought he might sink his cock into her overheated body, but he didn't. He went back to where he'd left off, four fingers in her pussy, his thumb circling her ass, rubbing at her hole. Dji was even kissing her stomach—she was surrounded by him.

Dji didn't breach her ass. Instead he eased his fist an inch at a time into her cunt. Ive was putty in his hands. There was a sharp pain that faded to pure pleasure. She was whimpering and making sounds she'd never made before, grunting, primitive noises. Her body clenched around his fist as he pumped it in and out.

Ive tossed her head from side to side—it was so—big, the moment was bigger than anything—ever, in her life. The only thing that would make it better would be his mating bite.

"More, please—I need more. Dji!" She screamed his name when he opened his hand inside her before easing back out.

She shivered, but wanted more, it still wasn't enough. Dji thrust his cock into her and pressed her down on the bed with his body—the weight adding another dimension. Her climax went on and on—Dji thrust a few more times and she couldn't stop touching him. Any skin she found, she caressed. She clutched him tight to her and wrapped her legs and arms around his body—thrusting back. She was peaking again, if it were possible.

"Ive!"

"Dji!"

He twitched a few times before collapsing on her and rolling to the side. Dji cuddled her close and stroked her back. Ive couldn't stop shaking.

"Are you okay?"

Ive couldn't even answer him with words. She nodded against his shoulder.

"Shh—" Dji continued to keep her next to him and whispered nonsense words into her ear, bringing her slowly back down.

When she could finally speak again, she had questions.

"Dji?"

"Hmm."

"You didn't—um—why didn't you bite me?"

Ive turned so she could look at him. She didn't want to ruin the moment, but she had to know. For months, hell, closer to years she'd dreamed of having her mate bond with her.

"It's too soon. What if I'm not whole? I don't want to leave you marked and alone if I have to leave. You deserve better."

"Shouldn't I be in on that decision? It's my life too." Ive sat up and crossed her arms over her breast.

"Ive—if something goes wrong I might have to be put down. If we don't mate there's a chance you could find someone else."

"I don't want anyone else." Ive glared at Dji.

"Things change. Just give me a couple weeks to adjust and if I don't have any residual signs of Dmitri we'll mate fully. For now—let me give you this." Dji pulled her to him and kissed her.

She couldn't help herself, she melted into the kiss, her mouth opening to allow Dji's tongue entrance. Tomorrow would have to be soon enough to fight for him. She knew in her heart that Dmitri was well and truly gone. The change in Dji was visible. Maybe she'd give him the week he wanted, but they didn't call her the Ice Queen for nothing. She was going to have her way and he would be hers. They belonged together and he deserved to be happy after the hell he'd been put through for centuries.

"I love the way you taste," Dji murmured against her lips.

They were breathing the same air. It was just as intimate as having a part of him so deep inside her she'd feel it for days.

"This doesn't let you off the hook." Ive stared deep into his eyes and they continued to sit there with their foreheads pressed together, gazing at each other.

"Fair enough. I don't know about you, but I'm tired and we have a meeting in the morning." Dji fought with the tangled blankets, then slid beneath them.

Ive followed suit. The travel and the phenomenal sex had taken it out of her. She didn't even really want to argue. Those who knew her would be shocked that she'd let it go, and she curled around Dji with her head on his chest, listening to the steady thump of his heart.

Chapter Nine

Dji looked around the room filled with strangers. The memories from Dmitri still resided in his head and some of these people looked familiar but he didn't really *know* them. Zareb and his mate Joy walked into the room and all eyes seemed to be drawn to them. Joy was flushed a pretty red. She had nothing to be embarrassed about. Ive had almost made them late with her shower. She loved the water and he was finding a new respect for it.

Once Zareb and Joy had settled onto a couch with another couple, the pack leader Russ spoke.

"Now that we are all here we can begin." Russ grinned in Zareb's direction. "For the record I would like to state that I *am* the alpha here. I know there were some questions before the group of you went to Africa, but I'm in charge. There may be members in here stronger than I am in the magic realm, but that doesn't make me weak."

Dji wasn't sure what Russ was speaking about. The leader didn't look weak to him. He exuded power and calm. Dji would follow Russ. Zareb seemed to have much faith in the wolf.

"It is how it should be. As I have stated before, the alpha should not have a guardian's power. Too much, and it could corrupt the best of us." Zareb spoke and Dji couldn't agree more.

There was no way he'd want to be the leader. Look what had happened to him—a strong alpha wouldn't have let himself be possessed. Just another of his failures.

"Well put, Zareb. I also want to reassure everyone on Djimon's presence. The man here in this room is *not* the one who was against us. That soul was named Dmitri and is no longer a threat. Most of you know this, but I wanted to reinforce it. Zareb, please fill us in on what happened." Russ gave Zareb the floor.

Dji watched Zareb bow his head towards the alpha in respect before speaking. "Our trip was not as uneventful as we had hoped. The plane crashed in the middle of the jungle, killing our pilot. We had to leave him and the plane. We should inform his family." Zareb looked towards Russ and at the alpha's nod he continued. "Once on the ground we moved as fast as we could, but were ambushed. They separated Joy and me from Dji and Ive. I believe that is because they thought Djimon was still Dmitri and they wanted to rescue him from us—he had followers in Africa. Ive and Dji will have to fill you in on that part of the journey. Joy and I managed to keep the Vessel with us."

"So nothing escaped from the vase?" The woman next to Joy spoke. Dji believed it was Joy's sister Valerie, but he wasn't a hundred per cent sure of everyone's name.

"Unfortunately that is not the case. Dmitri's soul tried to escape, but it was unsuccessful. We ran into an old tribe mate who managed to survive the carnage when Dmitri first emerged, Baakir. He came back with us."

"Yeah, we should keep an eye on him," Joy interrupted.

"Why is that?" Russ looked between Zareb and Joy.

Dji could understand the hesitation to completely trust Kir, but he should fall into that category too. After all—not too long ago Dmitri had tried to kill everyone in the room.

"He was influenced by Dmitri and the Vessel, but in the end he helped us. But Joy is correct, we should keep an eye on him. He might need help as well, getting used to a new life," Zareb answered.

"Then we'll see what we can do. I am assuming that the Vessel has been disposed of?" Russ questioned.

"Yes, Joy and I made sure it was sealed and Djimon added some extra power to the ground. We both think it would be good to send someone to the burial spot periodically to check the barrier." Zareb confirmed.

"I concur. I'll send pairs starting next month." Russ agreed.

It relieved Dji that Russ took the situation seriously. No one should go through the hell he had and, if they could prevent such a happening, the world would be a better place.

"I think that would be wise, Russ. It might be nice to have the shifters here see where they came from." Zareb sounded excited.

Dji would need time to come to terms with his homeland and its magic before he would return. If he could help it, he never wanted to go back to the spot where the Vessel was buried. Not that he'd be tempted to dig the thing up, but he still worried he could be possessed again.

"Africa is very rich in magic. I wouldn't mind going back, as long as I had access to a decent bathroom, or a car. I don't think I want to ever walk again," Joy piped up.

Valerie laughed.

"Zareb, you can help me with a rotation schedule. It might be nice for the magic users to go first." Russ looked over towards the couple on the couch next to Joy and Zareb.

"Oh, hell, no. Aren't Max and I the only magic users who *haven't* been?" Valerie looked horrified.

Now it was Joy's turn to laugh. "You'll be fine, V."

"Says you, the person who probably won't have to go back." Valerie crossed her arms across her chest.

"Is there anything else we should discuss?" Russ' gaze touched everyone in the room.

"I think we are safe for now. The Ancients have not spoken to me since our return. I am unsure if that is a good sign or a bad one. I will try to commune with them and let you know what they have said. There was a hint that our world could be exposed to humans, but I think we took care of that when the Vessel was destroyed."

Dji sure hoped so. The only thing worse, to him, than being possessed was having the humans exposed to shifter life. Being a science project wasn't on any of their agendas.

"Then this meeting is adjourned."

They all began filing out of the room. Dji followed Ive.

"Dinner isn't for a while, I don't think. We could go for a walk around the grounds."

"I think I'd like to think for a bit. Maybe you could talk to your friend — Vivian."

He thought that was the name of the princess of her tribe. They'd spoken of her a little when they'd woken up.

Ive's eyes watered and her forehead crinkled. He'd hurt her. He hadn't meant to, but it was time to decide if he should stay or not. It might be better for him to go off on his own away from the pack. He could cause more harm than good. He had to think of Ive's future.

Not something he'd ever had to do. Sure, Dji was charged with protecting his tribe, but a mate was another matter altogether. If something happened to her he might as well give up. And *he* could be the thing that happened.

"Sure. Yeah — find me later?"

Dji nodded and left the house. He didn't go far. The porch swing on the veranda would do the trick. He pushed against the ground and let the swing go back and forth. There was a light breeze. The pack house was truly magnificent. The wooded area alone was wonderful. Dji could imagine runs through those magical-looking trees. He'd like to explore the land more, if he stayed.

That was the big question. On one hand, he had the support of people who seemed on the ball. The core group in the meeting were all strong. Most in magic, but others in shifting power. They were connected. Even he could see that. The Ancients must have a plan he wasn't aware of. They hadn't talked to him once Dmitri had taken over.

What should I do? Are you there, Ancient ones? A sign would be nice.

No one answered, but he should have expected that. His faith wasn't the strongest right now. Dji wasn't alone for long. He felt another presence. One he recognised. Zareb was there.

Is this my sign?

"Where is Ive?" Not the question he'd expected, but easy to answer.

"I needed some space." Dji didn't even bother to look up.

"If that is your hint to leave you alone, it will not work. You should know me better than that, my old friend."

"I should be dead," Dji whispered.

And he should. The carnage he'd caused in their first tribe still gave him nightmares. He'd done that. His body had been responsible and his soul hadn't been strong enough to withstand an evil possession. Some protector he'd made. Killing a whole tribe wasn't keeping them safe.

"There will be no talk like that. It was not you in charge of those happenings," Zareb reassured him, but it didn't really help. They were just words.

"I was there. I could sense what was happening. If you'd been possessed, you would have fought harder and won. I think that is why Dmitri picked me. I'm weak."

"Enough. I will not have you speaking of my brother that way. Not when it should have been me. You were always the better person." Zareb sat down next to Dji.

"When I was trapped, I tried to escape, but I wasn't strong enough. There's no doubt about that. It was only after I was exposed to Ive that things came into focus."

"It was fated. You should know how the Ancients work."

The Ancients. Where were they in all of this mess? Always a voice and never any actual help. They always spoke in riddles that you had to figure out. Dji had never had a strong connection with the deities. It was supposed to strengthen when the final ceremony took place, but all hell had broken loose and it had never happened for him.

"Then, if it was fated, you have no call to feel guilt." Dji stood his ground.

It wasn't Zareb's fault that Dji had a defective soul.

"But I do because it was I who led you to that Vessel and I do not like that you call yourself weak. You are one of the strongest men I know. You have survived and you have a mate now," Zareb tried to reassure him.

"I won't be claiming her." Dji shook his head.

He didn't know when he'd come to that conclusion, but he knew it was the right answer. He had much to atone for.

"What does Ive have to say about that?" Zareb raised a brow.

"I—" Dji looked up at Zareb.

He didn't even want to face his mate, but he wouldn't take the coward's way out. He'd leave that night after dinner and hope he could face Ive and not run like the gutless man he was.

"Do not punish yourself. Do you know what Ive did for you? Did she tell you how she came to be here?"

"I'm not worthy."

Zareb stood and glared down at him.

"You will stop this now. I will not see you belittle who you are. You are Djimon, my brother, the protector, my friend and Ive's mate."

"Those are just words. I have been inside looking out, I'm not who I once was."

"You do not have to be. Find yourself and let Ive help. She put herself on the line for you. If not for her, you would be dead. Go to her, make right by her. Then come find me because I *do* want to get to know you, help you to find yourself again—and Kir is here as well. That is something—for the first time my family is here. In all my years of fighting with Dmitri I could never dream there would be a day some of my tribe would be near me. Do not make me lose that again so soon." Zareb kissed Dji on the forehead and left him.

It was a lot to think on. He'd been determined to leave, but now he was thinking of staying—this back and forth was just like something he would do. Would he ever feel like himself again and not this head case who couldn't make up his mind?

Lunch was announced. It was time to go speak to his mate. Or, maybe—after lunch would be better.

Ive wasn't hard to spot. She was a beacon of light to him. Talking seriously could wait.

"Did you have a nice time with Vivian?" Dji pulled out a chair for Ive.

"It was good. How was your time alone?"

"Zareb interrupted me and we spoke for a bit. It was nice talking to my brother."

Dji noticed that Pete had sat down beside him. Grey wasn't far behind.

"Where have you been all day?" Grey was seething.

Pete was staring down at the table not talking. Grey sat and Pete stood, leaving the dining area.

Grey stared after him but didn't move to follow. They seemed to be having as much trouble as he was.

"Grey—it'll be okay." Ive soothed her brother, but looked at Dji.

He figured the words were for both of them. Tonight wasn't going to go well. He could feel it in his bones.

Chapter Ten

Dinner wasn't too bad. Mostly small talk. Ive could see that Grey wanted to leave, but forced himself to stay. The road wouldn't be easy for her twin. Hell, it wasn't easy for her. In her gut, she knew Dji was on the verge of leaving the pack. She was strong and would live through his abandonment, but she didn't want to.

Kir was on their other side sitting beside a woman Ive hadn't been introduced to.

"Hello. I don't think we've met. I'm Ive and this is my mate Djimon." Ive held out a hand.

"Hi. I'm Naomi. Nice to meet you. You're the fox shifter, right? Part of Russ' mate's den?"

"That's right." Ive smiled.

"That's great. Are you planning on staying?"

Ive looked to Dji, but he seemed lost in thought. If he left, would she stay? It would probably depend on her brother.

"I think so. I like it here and Vivian is staying."

"Right. And your brother too. Pete is his mate, right? Sorry, I shouldn't gossip."

"No, no, that's all right. Yes, they're mates, but I have a feeling Pete is fighting it."

"He's had it rough. His damn parents should be shot." Naomi shared.

The men were being quiet. Ive didn't know if they were following the conversation or not. Kir kept sneaking glances at Naomi.

Would they all find mates in the Master's pack? It seemed so unlikely, but some force had brought them all together under one roof. Now, if the men would stop fighting it and be happy, things would be peachy.

Ive didn't hold any illusions. Her road wasn't any smoother than her brother's. Maybe for different reasons, but trouble still lay ahead.

Kir stood to leave and Naomi was quick to follow after saying goodbye.

"We should head to our room as well." Dji stood and helped her out of her chair. They dealt with their dishes and were leaving when there was a commotion at the door.

"I can't do this. No. I have to leave." Kir looked panicked.

Ive wondered what Naomi had said to him that had spooked him.

"I—I agree." Dji spoke softly, but Ive heard every word.

She couldn't breathe. He didn't mean… But he did.

"What the hell? We deserve a chance, Dji." Ive's eyes began to well. She rubbed at them.

"Ive—"

"Don't 'Ive' me. Stay and fight for me—for us. You've just come out of something traumatic, don't rush into a decision you'll regret. Give us time."

Dji's shoulders slumped, but he didn't answer. With one look at Kir, they left the room and walked through the door.

Ive collapsed in the hallway. She didn't care who saw. Tears streamed down her face. She'd thought she'd have time to convince him that they were meant to be. Enough of this shit. He couldn't run away. He needed to let her in and running away wasn't going to help. She stood and took a stunned Naomi by the hand.

"Come on. We're going to go talk to Zareb. They can't do this."

"I'm sorry. So sorry. I shouldn't have told Baakir we were mates. Men freak out about that right? And he's new here, we'd just met. I screwed up."

"Let's fix this."

Ive had to ask someone where Zareb's house was so they could get there. Maybe he'd have time to do…something. Tears welled up again and Ive dashed them away. It took a while for someone to answer her knock. She hoped it wasn't Joy. Joy already looked down on Ive. Her sister-mate wasn't the most flexible person and they tended to rub each other the wrong way. And now it looked like they had another sister-mate. The three of them were mates to the first created shifters. They needed to be strong. And hopefully over time they could bond.

Zareb opened the door.

"They're gone." Ive didn't even give Zareb a chance to say anything.

He held the door open and ushered them inside. Joy walked into the living room. It looked like they'd interrupted something. Joy's shirt was mis-buttoned and her hair looked—rumpled, for lack of a better word. Shoot, it just wasn't her day.

What's going on?" Joy looked between the three.

"Baakir and Djimon are gone." It hurt to even say it.

"Gone? Where?" Joy seemed confused. "For how long?"

Naomi broke in, taking over for Ive. "I was with Kir, talking to him after dinner. Djimon and Ive were leaving the room. Kir said something about not being able to do this. To—be here. Or talk to me, I guess." Naomi cleared her throat before continuing. "Djimon said he agreed with Kir. That's when they both took off."

"But they are together?" Zareb wanted to know.

"As far as we know," Ive acknowledged.

"What would make Kir run? Dji would take the littlest excuse to leave. Sorry, Ive, but he feels guilt over the things Dmitri did in his name."

The room went quiet. Naomi cleared her throat, but no one said anything as the tension grew in the room.

"Oh, fuck. Naomi, you and Kir are mates, aren't you?" Joy ran a hand down her face. "What is with this tribe and this splurge of mating going on?"

"Is this true?" Zareb looked at Naomi.

"It's my fault." Naomi's shoulders sank down low like she was trying to curl in on herself.

"Believe me, honey, none of this is your fault. Zareb's brothers are stubborn and loaded to the gills, or should I say whiskers, with guilt," Joy interrupted.

"What she says is true. It is not your fault." Zareb was quick to agree with his mate.

"But it was. I blurted out that we were mates. Then Djimon showed up and Kir bolted."

Joy guided Naomi farther into the house and pushed her onto the couch before leaving the room. She came back shortly with what Ive assumed was water, and handed it to Naomi.

"Ive, do you want anything?"

"No, sister-mate." Ive sat down next to Naomi and took her hand.

"Okay then, what's the plan of action?" Joy rubbed her hands together.

"I do not know. I spoke with both Dji and Kir today and told them that they belonged here, for them to think about that. I wanted my family whole again and I—maybe I pushed too hard." Zareb looked down at his hands.

Great, now she'd made Zareb feel guilty. She was batting a thousand today.

"Stop. This guilt thing you guys have going is making me sick. We're going to start living from today. No more of your past is going to interfere if I have to beat it into all of your heads. Ive, have you and Djimon mated yet?"

Ive's face heated. "We've had—done—but—haven't—that is, no we have not technically mated." Ive was beyond embarrassed. She didn't like to talk about her private life. Even if it was in the company of family. Especially in the presence of family.

"So you've done the mattress mambo, but no biting. Shit. I was hoping we could use that to locate him. Do you have something of his that we could use? I could try a spell maybe?" Joy glanced over at Zareb.

"Sometimes I can speak to Djimon in my mind. I have done it before, when Dmitri had possession," Zareb informed the group.

"Then what're you waiting for?" Joy seemed excited, like that would be the easy fix.

"It will take a moment. I need to centre myself. I will go outside." Zareb didn't wait for a response—he left the house.

"Can I get either of you anything?" Joy seemed a bit uneasy. As if she wasn't used to guests.

"No, I'm really sorry we barged in here. I really shouldn't even be here." Naomi bit her lip.

"Nonsense, we're family and it's about time that Djimon and Baakir realised they aren't alone anymore. It's hard when your family leaves you, but if there are others willing to fill the void you let them. I learned that the hard way." Joy shrugged. "Ive. Um—sister-mate?"

"Yes, Joy."

"I want us to be friends." Joy rushed the words out.

"I would like that, too." Ive reached out for her and the three women connected.

"I think the three of us are going to need each other. Our men are a little different than the others in the pack. They have more baggage and we're going to have to see them through it, all of us." Joy sent a pointed look at Naomi.

"I found them." Zareb had returned.

"Good, where are they?" Joy asked.

"They did not go far. They went to the clearing I took Kir to this afternoon. They will return in the morning. It seems the two of them have had a talk. Kir was set to go back to Africa until he told Djimon that Naomi was his mate. Dji refused to leave after that, told Kir that the guilt would not ruin them. I hope that is the case."

Ive couldn't hold it in anymore. Today had been a rollercoaster of unknowns. She sobbed into her hands. Naomi hugged her and stroked her back, calming her down.

"It'll be okay, Ive. Leaving like they did was a good thing. Being here is an even better thing. Knowing we can reach out to each other is a godsend. You shouldn't bottle things up so much. This weekend we're having a girls' night. We'll kick the guys out and let them do whatever in the main house and I'll invite all the women down here for a barbeque." Joy broke into Ive's cry fest. She almost didn't hear her.

"I—I would like that." Ive threw herself at Joy.

They stumbled, but Zareb was there to catch them. The support would be wonderful. So much better than her den. There had been so much hatred between the foxes. They were elitist and species snobs. They'd hated Grey and everything he stood for. There was no way they could go back now, not that they wanted to. She wondered how her brother was faring.

"It's settled then. Will you talk to Vivian? She should be able to arrange everything, being Russ' mate. Tell her I'll see her about it tomorrow." Joy patted her on the back.

"Thank you. We should go now." Ive wiped her face and gave Joy another squeeze before they left.

Dji and Kir sat on a log in a peaceful clearing. He shouldn't have left Ive like that. It hurt far worse than what he'd been expecting. Zareb had left a bit ago, but his words still stood between him and Kir.

If you both do not return I will find your mates suitable men in your absence.

That was what he wanted. Ive would be better off without him. But hearing those words aloud were his undoing. He'd already told Kir he couldn't leave his mate and he wouldn't be a hypocrite.

"We were wrong to leave, Kir. It was a hasty thing to do and we hurt two of the people who should be the most important in our world. I think that makes us selfish. You panicked and I followed suit." Dji sighed.

"I—Djimon, I went from having nothing and fighting for scraps to this—this—family? Now I'm expected to mate. It is very overwhelming."

"I know, but I guess that's what family is for. To help with the freak-outs. Now we have to hope we didn't screw things up too bad. No one is saying you have to mate right now. Get to know this woman. What was her name? Naomi?"

"Yes. The most beautiful woman I've ever seen."

"And you were going to leave that?"

Kir shrugged. "I panicked."

"Things haven't been easy for either of us. I think it's about time we did something about that. Don't you?" Dji felt stronger, now that he'd actively decided to stop being afraid and listen to his heart. Ive was his and he wasn't letting her go. He should be fighting for her, not running from her.

"Should we really let them wait all night?" Kir picked at his fingers and stared into the distance.

"No. We need to head back to the pack house. It's about time we got our new lives in order." Dji stood.

"Agreed. I'm only sorry I dragged you with me."

"None of that. I think we have enough guilt between us to power the world."

Kir chuckled. "You could be right.

Dji slapped Kir on the back. "Now let's hope our mates will listen to us.

Chapter Eleven

Pete wondered when Grey would catch up with him. He wasn't ready to talk. Not yet. His family problems were still at the forefront of his mind. He was seeing things that weren't there. Last night he'd gone outside and searched the area he'd thought his parents were at, but there was nothing there. Not even a good scent.

He would have to confront them or go crazy. It had been a long time since they'd been in his life. It was almost as if, once he'd joined the Masters' tribe, they'd left him alone. He'd always wondered if Ev had had anything to do with that. He should probably ask.

Grey cornered him on the stairs. He'd been going down and planned on taking a walk in the grounds to clear his head.

"I just wanted to tell you I'm packing up and heading out in the morning."

"Stay," Pete whispered.

"Why? Fuck you, Pete. I've tried—God, everything, and you keep pushing me away. I—fuck—I can't do this anymore, Pete. I can't." Grey slumped his shoulders, letting his head hang down.

He wouldn't even look at Pete anymore. He had to get closer, to somehow make Grey understand.

"I—"

"That's right. You. It all comes down to you and what you want and what you need and how things should be. No. I refuse. No more. I'm off the Peter train. I'll take my own den over you ripping my heart out every day and stomping on it for good measure. It's all or nothing time, babe. I'm not your fuck toy."

"Grey—please, listen I need time." Maybe if he'd explained about his parents Grey would understand and not leave.

"Your time just ran out, sweetheart." Grey didn't even look back as he stormed out of the pack house.

Pete didn't move.

"What the fuck are you doing, man? Go after him. Now." Ive pushed him towards the door.

He had no idea where she'd come from and it looked like she'd been crying. Naomi was with her and she looked just as bad as he felt.

Pete stumbled. "You heard him, Ive. It's over." He turned and headed to his room.

"You're an idiot," she shouted after him.

"What did you say?" Pete paused and looked back at Ive.

"I said—you're an idiot. My brother loves you. The two of you are mates—you both know it. Why are you fighting it so hard?"

"There are things—"

"Who gives a shit? Things don't matter when you've found the person who is the other half of your soul. I could have given up so many times. I mean—come on, my mate was possessed and had no control over himself for centuries, but that didn't stop me. He was mine and I would keep him at any cost. I would be broken without him. So stop whining and go get my brother." She pointed towards the door.

"You heard the lady — go." Russ demanded.

He hadn't even seen the pack leader show up.

"But, Russ — we're men — we shouldn't — "

"Don't care. He's your mate. That is all that matters. If it wasn't meant to be, the bond wouldn't be there. But it is. Now go get him and bring him back so our pack can finally settle down without the drama and become a family again."

Could he do this? Be everything Grey needed and more? Pete sat down on the stairs leading to the bachelor rooms upstairs. His room, where he would be so lonely with nothing to look forward to, but watching other mated couples being happy. Was he throwing it all away? And for what? Because his birth pack beat the shit out of him and called him an abomination? They wouldn't win. Not this time. He was home now in the Masters' pack and they loved him for being Pete, not where he stuck his dick or because of who he loved. And he did love Grey.

"I love him," he whispered in awe.

"Then get your ass out there and bring him back." Ive was standing in front of him.

Pete grabbed the railing and pulled himself up, rushing past Ive and Russ to the door. It was time to take his future in his own hands and stop living in the past. He flung the door open, looked down the path and didn't see Grey. He couldn't have gone far. Pete could smell better in his wolf form. He tossed his clothes off as fast as he could. The shift was over before he knew it. Pete sniffed and there it was — the most wondrous scent he'd ever smelt. Grey. The trees blurred as he picked up speed and didn't stop until Grey was in front of him and then howled before charging. He jumped and Grey caught him before they both fell to the ground.

He shifted back to his human form and wrapped his naked limbs around Grey.

"Stay," he whispered again. "I'm tired of being so alone. Don't go. Stay."

"That isn't what I want to hear, Pete."

"Grey, I love you, you stubborn fox. Let me redeem myself. Mate with me. Here. Now. I know we're technically already bonded, but let's make it stronger. I want to give you the words."

"Are you nuts? Pete—God, what you do to me."

"I—I'm scared. Fuck that was hard to say, but it's the truth. I ache for you and want us to truly bond, but I'm fucked up, babe. You make me whole, but I'm afraid this is all a dream and I'll wake up to my old tribe using me as an example. The things they did—no one should endure that and—I'm stronger than that now, because of you. But it won't be easy, Grey."

"I love you too, stupid. And of course it won't be easy, but that's why we have each other. Are you serious? You and me—fully mated?"

Pete looked down at Grey—this was his heart, his soul and the reason he was put on this Earth.

"Yes. Now you have too many clothes on."

"We are not doing this out here!"

"Why not?"

"For one—I'm pretty sure I can see my sister and half the pack coming this way. Two—no way am I binding myself to you outside in front of the house. Now if it was the woods—maybe, but not here."

"Okay. You're right, but I don't want to mate with you in my room. Too many people."

"Shift and follow me. I have the perfect spot."

Pete didn't change, not yet. He had to know, because he figured after the way Grey had left he'd have more of a fight on his hands to win his man back. He'd chased him fully prepared to grovel.

"It's that easy?"

"Stop being scared. I've got you and no one is going to hurt you again. All I wanted was for you to say you love me and wanted to be more than fuck buddies in spite of some fucked-up things that happened with your old tribe. You're here and say you're giving it your all. You want us together. I'm not going to play hard to get because you were mine the moment I met you. Do you remember? You let me into the pack house intent that I should wait in Russ' office, but I charged into the kitchen. I couldn't take my eyes off of you. Then you insisted on following me to protect Russ and Vivian. You're so much stronger than you think you are. You protected me even when you fought us being mates. And your fuckin' cousin, Everett, didn't help matters."

"Hey!" came a shout from behind them.

Pete grinned. There was Ev, not that he should have been surprised. Ev was always there for him when he needed it. "We really should take this somewhere else."

"Yes, but I was having fun reminiscing about the time we were on the run."

"We can have a flashback moment later. Yes, I know you wanted me even then. I wanted you too, but I wasn't ready. I'm ready now." Pete shifted.

Grey hadn't thought he'd ever be this happy. He'd gone from heartbreak to euphoric in minutes. He'd thought he'd lost his very soul. It had been ripped out and he hadn't thought he'd be whole again until Peter had tackled him. And now he was sitting around talking when he could be bonding with the man who meant everything to him.

He looked down at the wolf sitting waiting patiently for him and smiled. He closed his eyes for a moment, overwhelmed at what he'd almost lost. When he opened them again it was to see Ive, Max, Vivian and Everett walking back to the house. There were other members of the pack, but those four people were the most important to him. Everett and Max for taking such great care of his mate when he'd had no one else and Vivian for being the sister of his heart, and of course Ive—his soul. Walking this path to a new beginning would be different. They weren't the most important people in each other's lives anymore, but they would always be there for each other.

Ive winked and tugged Everett back down the path, the others following. He'd have to see what he could do about getting Everett mated—someone who would drive the wolf to distraction.

A howl brought him back to himself, reminding him that he still had clothes on. That wouldn't do. In seconds he was shifted to his fox form. He was startled when something dropped beside him. Everett had got away from Ive and tossed something. Grey went to see what it was and if he'd been in human form he would have grinned. Lube. He yipped and picked it in his mouth before racing to a secluded spot deep in the wood where no one would find them. Pete followed close beside him, never strayed too far.

Finally he got to the spot he wanted. There was a pond, and trees surrounded the area. It was magical. Grey dropped the lube and changed to his human form. Pete transformed as well. They lay side by side staring up at the night sky.

"I need to say something before we start. I didn't learn this bonding ritual in my tribe. It wasn't until Russ took me in that I learned the basics. I think my parents hated me from the very beginning, and me telling them I was gay made it worse. The night I told them, they beat me within an inch of my life. I was lucky to get out of there."

Grey bristled. If he ever saw Pete's parents he would tear them limb from limb. Who did that to a kid? Sure, most of his tribe had had a beef with him, but he'd held his own and had always had Ive. Their parents didn't care and loved them both unconditionally.

"I did some things I'm not proud of and it took me a while to find my cousin. Ev is like the brother I never had and vouched for me. Russ didn't hesitate. Just like that—I was family. It takes me a while to trust and then you show up. So cocky and sure of yourself. And you wanted me."

Grey wanted to stop Pete, but knew his mate had to tell his story. "It's okay. Just get it out and know—I love you no matter what. I don't care about your past and I want to kill your parents, but I'm here for you. For that matter, so are Ive and Vivian."

"I know—my head does at least—it's just taken my heart a while to catch up. I freaked last night because I thought I saw my parents outside. It was a trick of the light, but every time I've ever shown any interest in someone they were there. I panicked. I'm sorry. I had to get my head on straight and needed to think. Then you tell me you're leaving. I couldn't fuck it up. Not this. I was so close to having everything I wanted. I think—I think I need to go see them."

"No!" Grey sat up and stared down at Pete.

"Yes. I think you should come too. I need to make sure they stay away. I don't want to be looking over my shoulder all the time."

"I'll go, but I'm not promising I'll behave."

"Duly noted." Pete sat up too and pulled Grey to him. "Now—I think there was talk of strengthening our bond. Are you ready?"

"What do we need to do? In our tribe we just bite and release the mating serum—which I didn't do in Africa—just so you know. There's more for you, right? I heard about a ritual and some words?"

"I didn't think you'd do that to me, even when I was a bit spazzed, I had faith in you. And there is so much more to the wolves' way of taking a mate. Why don't we mate your way first then we'll get your ass ready and I'll show you what I was taught. I just hope I remember it all."

Chapter Twelve

Pete was nervous. Things seemed to be going his way. Happiness was in his grasp and he was going to take it with both hands.

Grey kissed him and the world faded away. It was the two of them in a cocoon of happiness. Cheesy, sure, but he was allowed. Pete was in love, with a man. He was gay and had a mate. His parents were wrong.

"I'm doing something wrong if you're thinking that hard." Grey bit him where his shoulder joined his neck.

There was no warning at all. Grey's fangs pricked his skin and Pete's cock got harder than it ever had before. He didn't know he'd be into biting, but the sensation was wonderful and his body warm. It might have something to do with knowing they were making the bond they'd started in Africa even stronger. Grey licked the abused skin and Pete tilted his head to give Grey more room.

"You could do that all night and I'd be happy."

"I wouldn't. You promised me a ritual."

"Right. Okay. It goes pretty fast and involves a lot of words, biting and sex. Think you can handle it?" Pete winked at Grey.

He laughed when Grey tackled him and started tickling him. Who knew sex could be fun. No one had ever told him. He had so much to learn and couldn't wait for Grey to teach him.

"I give! Uncle!" Pete laughed and Grey nuzzled into his shoulder.

Pete scraped Grey's throat with his teeth before sinking them into the tender flesh. He leant back and whispered the words, "You're mine, in mind."

The reverence wasn't lost on him. Nothing mattered but this moment in time. He licked his way to Grey's chest right where his heart was. He gave it a kiss before biting down. "You're mine, in heart." He whispered above the broken skin.

This time he kissed his way down to where Grey's thigh met his pelvis and again he bit down. "You're mine, in body."

Now it was time for the last part that would bind them together tighter than any other ceremony on Earth. Pete sank slowly into Grey saying the words, "You're mine now, in mind, heart and body forever more."

Grey moaned and threw his head back. The clearing swirled with magic and Pete could feel Grey even more strongly. They were one.

He tugged and was rewarded with Grey's orgasm. A clap of thunder echoed in the clearing and lightening flashed across the sky. Magic crackled in the air, even stronger now than when Pete had uttered the words.

Heat infused his body from head to toe and he shook. Grey fell on top of him, panting for breath. It couldn't have been more perfect if they'd been in a five-star hotel somewhere. The wildlife had started making itself known, but Pete wasn't ready to move. He held Grey close and peppered kisses on any part of Grey's body he could reach.

Perfect. There was no other way Grey could explain what had happened. The ritual was beautiful and much better than the bite the foxes would give. Their bond was as strong as it was going to be. The words must have been some kind of spell, because, even though he wasn't a magic user, he could feel it in the air.

Were the stars brighter? Maybe he was just in love.

"I love you, Pete." Grey kissed his chest.

He didn't want to move, but Pete had to be getting uncomfortable on the ground. They should go back to the pack house, but there were too many people. Maybe they should see about getting their own place on the pack land. So they could have their own home. Grey would like that. He'd suggest it to Pete — maybe tomorrow, no need to freak him out tonight.

It had been a big step and Grey realised that. His mate had been through too much in his life and Grey wanted to make their years together happy.

"I love you too, Grey."

"We should —" He couldn't finish the words because Pete squeezed him tight.

"Not yet. Please."

Grey couldn't deny Pete and it wasn't his back on the ground. He was content to lie on top of Pete all night. Who needed a bed? Covers would be nice, but they didn't even have their clothes. They'd shifted closer to the pack house. They'd have to shift again to get back. He was feeling a bit protective of Pete and didn't want anyone looking at him. It was silly, they all got naked when they ran as a pack, but he could be irrational right now. They were newly bonded.

He hadn't thought things could get stronger after Africa, but he'd been wrong. Grey listened to Pete's heart as it slowed down. Pete had started caressing his back. This is what he'd always wanted. A mate to share things with and now he had that. They might still have some issues, but now they could work through them together. And it wasn't as if Pete could really ever leave him. One of the perks of being mated was the ability to find your mate anywhere.

They could also tell how the other was feeling. Like right now, Pete was sleepy and content, even though they were both sticky and, a little cold. The breeze had picked up. Grey wasn't going to complain. They'd have to come back to this spot again. It was peaceful. Grey wondered if the other pack members knew about it.

His question was answered when a couple stumbled out of the woods.

"Oh!" the woman squealed.

Pete tensed up, but didn't move.

Grey didn't know who they were and didn't say anything yet.

"Sorry, Pete, we didn't know anyone was out here. We'll leave you guys—"

"No, it's okay. We were actually just leaving." Grey stood and reached down a hand to help Pete up. He stood in front of Pete, protecting him.

Pete smiled and nodded before shifting. Grey didn't have time to introduce himself to the couple because Pete had run off. He was going to give chase.

"Evening." He nodded and thought of his fox form and raced after Pete.

He caught up with him—Pete hadn't gone far and was waiting for him. Grey ran full tilt and bowled Pete over. If he'd been in human form he'd have laughed. They played for a few minutes before heading back. This—this was what Grey could get used to and he was very happy Pete was giving him a chance to live it. Yep, he was asking Russ about that house because he wanted to make Pete howl as often as possible. He nipped at Pete's legs and skidded to a stop at their clothes.

Ev was there waiting for them. Neither shifted and it didn't look like Ev needed them to.

"Pete—I'm happy for you man, you totally deserve all the happiness in the world. Grey—don't dick him over or I will hunt you down and you don't want to be on my bad side." Ev turned and left them alone.

Grey shifted back and watched his mate do the same, "Well, I can say this—he is very protective and I'm happy you had him, but now that's my job."

Grey gave Pete a hard kiss on the mouth before tugging on his clothes. Life would never be dull around this pack, but Grey was ready for the adventure.

Chapter Thirteen

"So you decided to come back tonight?" Ive turned on the bedside lamp.

She wasn't going to make this easy for him, but Dji hadn't expected her to. It was time to man up.

"We need to talk. I should have said that earlier instead of running off. I have no excuse. Kir told me Naomi was his mate and I was shocked that he wanted to go home. I made him stop and we talked. I realised I was being a hypocrite. I want to explore what we have. Tell me it isn't too late." Dji sat on the edge of the bed.

"I should tell you no and make you leave, but there is something you didn't take into account when you left. I've fallen in love with your dumb ass. If you hadn't come back of your own free will I would have come after you, make no mistake about it. I had my breakdown moment, but that's over. We're a partnership and you're going to have to deal with it.

"Dmitri might have had control of your body, but he never touched your soul. We both know it. If he had, you wouldn't have recognised me and you wouldn't have helped Valerie. You forget, I'm new here too. The only family I truly have is my brother. I need you as much as you need me."

His mate was so strong, but instead of saying she deserved better, maybe he should think of her as his strength.

"Things won't always be easy."

"You think it's been easy so far?" Ive raised a brow.

Dji threw back his head and laughed. "This is true. It took a lot to get here. I promise not to run away again and to talk to you if I need to."

"It doesn't always have to be me. You have your brothers, just as I have my sister-mates. The six of us are stronger together. I don't think the pack knows what they have in you — the protectors."

"We aren't protectors anymore. I've never truly been one. Kir was never meant to be one, but the magic used when the Vessel was opened changed that. He's been through his own hell."

"Then we're here for him and need to let him know. His mate is very upset. She thinks it's her fault the two of you ran off."

"I'll have to talk to her tomorrow. Kir will have a harder time adjusting to America and the idea of a mate is more than he knows what to do with. He hasn't really spoken of what happened, but I know he felt abandoned."

"Guess we'll have to show them the ropes." Ive winked.

She could break the tension with just a few words and a gesture. She really was his other half. She wouldn't let him get too serious and he'd have to return the favour.

Dji pushed Ive onto the bed. She was already naked. He hadn't noticed it before because she was under the blankets, but they had fallen away from her breasts, leaving the plump temptation in front of him. He took a nipple in his mouth and bit down. This time it was hard enough to draw blood. Ive almost came off the bed. Dji didn't let go. He released the mating serum and retracted his teeth, licking at the wound.

"Again. Please."

His little fox liked to be bitten. Something he'd have to remember. Dji went to the other breast and gave it the same treatment, biting down hard, as he released more fluid. Ive reared off the bed and sank her teeth into his neck. Dji's cock pulsed, his body was warmer than it had ever been.

They were now truly mated. He knew that this tribe had a ritual, he'd learned that through Dmitri, but his magic was strong enough that a bite would do it, and it looked as if it was the case with his mating to Ive. He would never leave her again. She was too important and he'd die before he left her side in a panic again. This was his life and he was going to live it like it was intended. To its fullest with the woman that meant the world to him by his side.

If someone had told him months ago that he'd be in this position—well, he wouldn't have done anything because he was trapped in his own body, but there was so much he wanted to do and see.

Ive kissed his shoulder and wrapped her arms around him.

"Dji, I need you."

Dji followed her onto the bed, pressing her down. The last time he'd done this she'd squirmed so he knew she liked it. He was pleased that she liked things a little rougher. Not that he'd always be that way with her. Like now—now was the time for soft and gentle. He was going to make love to his mate.

"I love you, Ive."

Ive almost cried again. She didn't think she'd hear those words. She'd despaired of ever hearing them. When he'd walked through the door she'd been so relieved. Now they were mated and he'd said he loved her.

"Make love to me, Dji."

She lifted her neck so their lips could meet. It was a gentle brush of mouths. Ive closed her eyes and enjoyed the moment. Dji nibbled along her jaw and licked at her neck. She was more sensitive there than she realised. Ive shivered and sighed. Her eyes still closed, she enjoyed each touch and caress. Dji lapped the mating marks he'd made. She thought most people bit the neck, but she liked this much better. Ive wondered if she could get him to do that again—later. Right now the soft touches of Dji's mouth were driving her crazy. Ive clutched the sheets. Dji was moving the top blanket completely off her to continue his tour of her body.

"Dji—I need you—please."

He wasn't listening, taking his time. He reached her pussy and she remembered their first time, his fist inside her. She wanted that again. It was so intense and better than anything she'd felt before. There would be time for that later as well. Right now she wanted Dji's cock inside her. He bit down on her clit— not too hard, but enough for her to dig her heels into the mattress and thrust into Dji's mouth. He licked and nibbled between bites. Ive squirmed on the bed. Dji stopped and Ive whimpered. She needed to come so bad, but he wasn't letting her. Every time she got close he stopped. It was frustrating, but she soon forgot it when he started back up again. Dji kept bringing her to the edge.

"Please," Ive panted. She didn't know what she wanted—for him to stop or keep going. She was out of her mind. Dji kissed his way up her body, his thumb taking over where his mouth had left off. He flicked her clit and not in rhythm she could get used to.

Dji reached her mouth and kissed her. Ive moaned into his mouth. He tasted like her. She bit at his lips, sucked on his tongue and wrapped her arms around his body, scratching at his back. She was going crazy.

Finally he gave her what she wanted. He spread her legs wide and thrust inside her. Ive held her legs back, giving him more room to move. His balls slapped her ass, adding another level to the experience. She wanted to suck on those balls, to have Dji's cock in her mouth. Even to taste herself on his length to see if it was different than from his tongue. The very idea excited her. She was surprising herself left and right. Ive never would have guessed she was kinky, but there was so much she couldn't wait to do with Dji.

"Harder—more," Ive panted.

He listened and thrust harder and harder. Ive wrapped her legs around him, digging her heels in to hold him in deep. She moved meeting his every stroke. She was so close.

Dji tweaked her nipples and that was it, Ive's body shuddered.

"Dji, Dji, Dji." Ive bit her lip and kept saying her mate's name over and over.

He tensed up and closed his eyes. He was coming deep inside her and they felt complete. It was her turn to sooth Dji. She caressed his back. Ive didn't want him to move, she enjoyed his weight on top of her, but he didn't stay that way for long. Dji turned them over so she could rest on his chest. Even now he was protecting her and she didn't think he even realised it.

"Where do we go from here?" Dji asked her.

"The shower?" Ive teased.

"I'm serious."

"So am I—and I'm sticky." Ive kissed the closest available skin, Dji's chin.

"All you ever think about is the shower."

"African jungle—that's all I have to say about that. I don't think I'll ever be clean enough."

"Okay, then, after the shower—what next?"

Ive wasn't in the mood to be serious. "Sleep? It's been an exhausting day. Grey almost walked off, you left. Yeah...I'm thinking sleep sounds mighty good right now."

"Ive—"

"We can be serious tomorrow. Tonight? Let's just wallow in the fact that we're mates. Maybe talk more about that fist thing you did." Ive winked.

"Oh, you liked that, did you?"

"Do you even have to ask? You were there when I came apart."

"I may have hated being possessed, but I did learn a trick or two." Dji smirked.

He seemed entirely too pleased with himself and Ive liked this look on him. Now she could see the man he must have been and she enjoyed him.

"Guess we have some exploring to do. Race ya to the shower." Ive hopped out of bed and dashed into the bathroom.

Dji's laughter followed her. She liked that even more and vowed to make him do it more often. People might call her the Ice Queen, but she had a heart. It had just taken Dji to thaw it out.

He wasn't too far behind her and she squealed when he picked her up and tossed her over his shoulder, slapping her ass.

"I win."

It was Ive's turn to laugh. In her mind, they'd both won and it made her smile. She'd travelled a great distance, but in the end it had been worth every mile. She wouldn't change a thing because she was right where she wanted to be. With her mate. Tomorrow they would talk to her brother and Naomi. The Masters' pack was the best thing that had ever happened to her and she would do what she could to protect them and her mate. Even if that meant protecting Dji from himself.

"I love you, Djimon, with every inch of my being." She kissed his back.

"I'm yours in every way and that doesn't scare me. Not anymore. I love you too."

"All right—let's hit the showers!" Ive slapped Dji's ass and he almost dropped her.

She laughed and everything felt right with the world. Not only had she gained a mate, but also an extended family that would be there when she needed them. It put her den to shame and she was overjoyed that they would be able to stay here and help the Masters' tribe thrive.

Dji would become the protector he was always meant to be and she would be right there by his side every step of the way.

Epilogue

Pete and Grey pulled up to his old pack house. Ive and Dji had insisted on coming and they'd almost had a car full when more of the Masters' tribe had insisted they should be there too. He was thankful his cousin Ev had come along as well. He really needed all the support he could get. He shouldn't have been surprised by all the support, the pack always came through. They were family and he was just now really starting to see that. It sucked that it'd had taken him so long to figure out his place in it.

The house didn't look as scary as it had in the past. Before it had been dark and looming and now — it just looked like a house. Being mated to Grey had put a lot of things into perspective for him. He wasn't an abomination and his family couldn't hurt him anymore.

He needed this confrontation on many levels so he could feel whole again. Russ, his alpha, led the way. Pete was choked up when he'd said he'd be coming too and that it was about time he put Pete's parents in their place. That's when it really clicked that he was in the place he needed to be.

They didn't have to come and he'd told them that. It was ultimately his fight, but he had a new family now and they would have none of it. He smiled when he remembered Ive yelling that she was his sister now and she'd damn well come if she wanted to, so she could beat some sense into the people who had almost kept Pete from Grey.

Life had completely changed for him. He was no longer the loner. Grey would drag him to the pack dinners or they'd have a nice evening in with Dji and Ive. Pete loved those nights the best. Ive was a spitfire and kept Dji in line and Dji was stronger than ever, he smiled more now and joked around. It had taken a couple of months for everyone in the house to feel comfortable with Dji, but not for Pete. They'd bonded the first night Ive had demanded they come over for dinner.

And Ive reminded Pete so much of his mate Grey. They shared a lot of mannerisms and would finish each other's sentences. Dji and Pete would just look on in amusement when they shared tales of their own dysfunctional den. It made Pete happy, knowing that the Masters' tribe was there for them all.

Russ was the best leader a person could have. He was fair and had never looked at Pete differently because he loved a man. It really didn't matter to Russ.

It was time. Russ stood at the door and knocked. Grey reached for Pete's hand, curled his fingers around Pete's and squeezed, not letting go. And it wasn't weird. Before, Pete would have snatched his hand away and been mortified of the public display, but no more. He was proud of his mate. He raised their hands and kissed Grey and, as luck would have it, that's when the door opened.

"Is your alpha here?" Russ' voice was strong and clear.

"Who are you and why's the fag here?" Pete knew that voice.

That was his own brother. It shouldn't have hurt, but it did. Pete had to hold Grey back because he was straining against him.

"He isn't worth it, love." Pete kissed his hand again and said nothing, letting Russ do the talking. A month ago he wouldn't have been so confident and would have cowered behind people at the anger coming from Don, but no more.

Russ bristled and Pete could feel the power roll over him. His brother, Don, whimpered. He was just happy that it wasn't directed at him even though he still had the urge to shift and show his belly.

"I asked for your alpha. Get him. *Now.*"

Don scrambled back and left the door open. Russ walked in and the group followed. Any confidence he had left him as he walked through the door. Grey stroked Pete's back and it was keeping him calm. He was about to hyperventilate — too many bad memories in the place. Pete could remember the beating he'd got by the stairs leading to the second floor. He'd been thankful he'd reached the bottom before his dad and brother had cornered him. That was right before they'd kicked him out, hoping he'd die.

There was a time Pete had hoped for that as well, but thanks to Ev and Russ that had changed.

His mother and father stormed into the living room.

"What the hell is going on here?"

Pete's father didn't even look at him, his focus was on Russ. There was no offer of a handshake or anything that remotely looked like hospitality. He took a minute to really look at the man who had made his life hell. His dad looked old and small, his once dark hair now a dingy grey. Pete noticed that his mom had a black eye. It shouldn't have surprised him—his father was a bully and no one was immune from his wrath.

"Mr Tyler, your son needed some closure and as the head of his pack I wasn't going to let him come by himself. We're his family now and we want you and your pack to stay away from him and his mate. Peter has told me some disturbing stories and I want to nip any retaliation from you in the bud here and now." Russ stood tall and stared Pete's father down.

When his father looked away, Pete relaxed. He couldn't hurt him anymore.

"His—*mate*? That abomination found a woman who would take him?"

Pete almost laughed, but he was still too freaked out about being there. His father really thought he'd end up with a female?

"Why would he have a woman as a mate? He's gay. No, his mate is standing right beside him." Russ pointed to Pete and Grey.

It was the first time his father had looked at him since rushing into the room. His mother cringed.

They can't hurt me anymore.

He only had to repeat it in his head a few times to feel better.

"What kind of alpha would let that freak live. He should be put down." Pete's father moved towards him like he would take care of it here and now.

And there went any calm his chant had given him. Grey moved in front of Pete, but it wasn't him that challenged Pete's father.

"That's enough, Uncle Roger. You can't hurt him anymore. Stay clear of our home, or you won't like the welcome you receive." Ev glanced away and stiffened at something in the corner.

Pete didn't have time to look and see what had drawn his attention. It was time to step up and cut all ties once and for all.

"Mr Tyler—" No way was Pete calling him dad. "I am no longer a member of your pack. Ties were cut a long time ago and you need to stop harassing me. I am happy and mated with a new pack and family. You can't hurt me anymore. I'm bigger and stronger now. This ends here."

He nodded to his mother then turned on his heels and went for the door. A crash made him look around. His father had made a move on him while his back was towards him. He had a knife in his hand. Where that had come from was anyone's guess. But now he was on the ground, Grey on top of him.

"You will never touch my mate again, you coward." Grey spat on the floor by Pete's father's head.

Grey kept the knife and returned to Pete's side.

"No one will ever hurt you again, babe." Grey kissed his temple.

Pete closed his eyes and savoured the love coming from his mate.

"Thank you."

"I love you, Pete."

"I love you too, Grey."

They walked out of the house as a group. The howl of rage from inside shut off when the door was closed. That chapter of Pete's life was over. He knew that, if his father tried to come after him, he had a full pack at his back and would never be alone again.

"Your old man is lucky I'm a lady. I was going to lay his ass out flat. Fucker." Ive squeezed Pete and walked ahead of him to catch up with Dji.

Grey laughed. "She isn't lying. She would have taken him out."

Pete smiled because he believed every word of it. Ev walked behind them with Russ. The two men were whispering. Pete turned around and was surprised to see Ev had three small blonde women with him. They looked shocked and were trembling a little. One had a broken arm, and the other two were bruised. It had to be the result of living with his father, but he'd never seen them before. They must have joined after he'd left. How his father kept getting new members he'd never know. By now most of the shifter world should have heard of his father's out of control temper and heavy hand.

Everyone stopped by the van.

"Ev brought something to my attention as we were leaving. These women need a new home and I think our tribe will be the perfect place for them." Russ and Ev helped them into the vehicle. The youngest one flinched at the touch. Pete was afraid to find out what they'd been through.

He just wondered how Ev had got them out and convinced them to go with them. Pete's father's hold was strong. It had to be, he didn't rule with heart like Russ, he ruled with an iron fist. Sometimes two. If anyone went against him, they were beaten. If he didn't do it his betas would. They were all cruel. He wished he had the power to disband them, but it wasn't his problem any longer.

"They'll need some time to heal. There is a cottage open at the edge of the property we'll get them settled into." Russ got into the van.

Ev started to get in too. Ive was in the front with Dji, and started the van. The women were in the rear of the van holding on to each other, leaving the middle seat for the rest. Russ slid back with the women, which was probably a good call. Being an alpha he had a way about him that would calm other shifters, something Pete's father had never had.

"Hey, Ev, how did you get them to come with you?" Pete raised a brow.

"Your dad is a fucker. I saw them huddled on the couch all beat to shit and went over to them while you were busy almost getting stabbed. Nice save by the way." Ev slapped Grey on the back. "I just told them if they wanted out to come with me, we were leaving. They didn't look back."

Ev glanced to the back seat and clenched his fist by his side. Pete had never seen him so angry before.

"You did good, cuz." Pete squeezed his shoulder.

"No one should have to be put through that. No one."

"That man should be put down," Grey agreed.

Pete didn't say much because he thought so too.

"You guys getting in sometime today or you just gonna stand there lookin' pretty." Ive shouted.

Ev actually blushed, mumbled something and got into the van.

"What was that about?" Pete mused.

"I think he likes one of the women." Grey winked.

Pete looked towards the back. He wondered what their story was and if they would ever find out. For Ev's sake he hoped it wasn't anything too horrible. It would be great if his cousin could find a mate of his own. Pete had never been so settled in his life and wished that for the only other man he loved with his whole heart.

He slammed the door shut and looked at his childhood home. It wasn't scary anymore. His father was a bully and an old man. Pete finally saw him for what he truly was. He leaned his head on Grey's shoulder and breathed in his scent. It was the only thing that could calm him no matter what.

The nightmares were still there sometimes, but they weren't coming like they used to. When they did, all he had to do was snuggle into his mate and breathe him in. It had been a draining day and he hoped the nightmares would stay away tonight. Maybe he'd have Grey help him get so tired that all he could do was sleep. He grinned, thinking of all the things they could do to pass the time.

Today truly was the first day of his new life. He'd stood up to his father, put his past behind him and embraced who he truly was and, if things went well, he'd have Ev mated and just as happy as he was.

Anything was possible if you grabbed life with both hands and never let go, he was living proof of that.

* * * *

Ive looked back at her brother as Dji drove the van. She was content. Something she'd feared might never happen. To have her brother settled was just one more thing to make her happy, and the Masters' pack was much better than the fox den. Here she felt like part of the group. She was even getting along better with Joy.

They'd had the girls' night out and, for the first time, she was comfortable in her own skin and had let down her guard. They didn't call her the Ice Queen anymore. At least not where she could hear it. Naomi was adjusting to Kir and he seemed to be taking his new life in his stride. He hadn't tried to run again. She thought having Dji and Zareb around helped. The girls had another outing scheduled. Shopping. Ive was looking forward to it because a girl couldn't have too many shoes.

Russ had even put her to use helping Dji and Zareb train the others to protect themselves, now that Vivian no longer needed her and Grey to protect her. Dji had told her that the Ancients were still concerned with the shifters being exposed to humans. Ive hoped with all her heart this wasn't the case. Their lives would never be the same again unless they controlled the information. She sighed. Maybe she'd bring it up to Russ. If the Ancients were worried it must be coming and soon. Someone had to have connections with the government to ease the world into the existence of the supernatural.

"What is it, my love?" Dji glanced at her then turned back to watching the road.

"I'm happy."

"That didn't sound like a 'happy' sigh."

He'd come to know her well.

"I'm also thinking of the future."

"That bad?" Dji grinned and reached over to squeeze her leg.

He smiled more often now and it still made her stomach flutter, his hand on her thigh didn't hurt either. Anytime he touched her she went up into flames. Now probably wouldn't be the time to bring that up—not with a van full of witnesses. No need to share her sex life with the whole pack.

"Just a bit worried."

It felt good to admit that. Most of the time she stayed too strong. With Dji—she didn't have to.

"Because of the prophecy?"

"How did you know? Anyways, does it have to be a prophecy just because they say? Can we prevent it?" Ive bit her lip.

"I can always tell what you're thinking." Dji took her hand and squeezed, she didn't take it away. His touch comforted her.

"So?" She insisted.

"It might be time to 'come out' to the humans. They are enlightened now. I saw a couple shows on television about vampires and shifters. They seem popular."

"That's what you think. Individual humans, sure, but get them together and it's mob mentality. We could end up locked up in a lab somewhere. Maybe we should see if Russ can talk to someone."

"Now I think it's you who has been watching too much television. Don't borrow trouble, Ive. When the time comes, we'll have each other. We'll get through this." Dji brought their hands to his lips and kissed her palm. "You've proven to me we can get through anything."

Ive looked back again to see Pete's head against Grey's shoulder. Grey winked at her and she turned around. Dji was right. She needed to live in the now because they were happy. The threat might be out there—but no one knew when. They could all be long dead before it came to pass. For now, she would enjoy having a family.

A shiver raced down her spine and goose bumps raised up on her arms. A breeze moved through her hair, but the windows were closed.

"It's coming."

Ive looked over at Dji, but he was focused on the road. What was coming? Who'd said that? It hadn't been him, the voice sounded different. It didn't even sound like one person...but a group of them just in her head. It wasn't a good feeling.

"Ive?" Dji looked worried.

"Nothing." She tried to shake it off. Maybe it was her overactive imagination.

Ive looked out of the window, but held on tight to Dji's hand.

"Everett and Kitty are the key."

She looked again—nothing. Ive turned completely around in her seat. Ev was looking at the women in the back and no one else seemed to have heard the weird voice, but something was coming. There went her vow to worry about the now.

There was no other explanation but the Ancients, and since when did they talk to her? She wasn't connected to them in anyway. The foxes didn't even worship the Ancients. They hadn't for centuries. It looked like she'd be called in to protect her family. No way was she giving them up. Once they got to the house she'd have to talk to Bella, the pack seer. Why weren't they talking to her anyway? Didn't they go always go to her or Zareb?

Pete would be devastated if something happened to his cousin, and Grey would go crazy if harm came to Pete. Couldn't they all catch a break? It seemed like the Masters' were up to their eye balls in hurt and pain with no clear break in sight.

And for that matter—who the hell was Kitty? Ive closed her eyes and laid her head on her seat. There was nothing she could do until they got home. What more could the universe throw at them?

Ive knew that she shouldn't ask because it would only cause more trouble. She didn't even notice how long the trip was—they were already home. She watched as the others got out of the van, but she didn't move. Dji waited as well.

Once everyone was out, Dji turned to her. "Something happened. Talk to me."

"The Ancients spoke to me."

"What did they say?" Dji looked worried.

He didn't even question why they were talking to her. She couldn't love him any more than she did in that moment.

"That something is coming and Ev and Kitty are the key."

"Who's Kitty?"

Ive threw up her hands. "That's what I wanted to know. And why is Ev the key?"

"I don't know, but we'll figure it out. Let's go inside. We'll talk to the others. I don't know about you—but I'm tired of these meetings." Dji sighed and released his seatbelt.

She chuckled and followed suit. They met in front of the van. He was so old fashioned. Dji held out his hand, ever the gentleman. She intertwined her fingers with his, the smallest connection made her happy.

"You do know they'll be busy for a while with the new members. We could go to our place—"

She threw her head back and let out a full bodied laugh.

"I like the way you think, Dji." She changed the direction they were going and tugged him along.

That's just what she needed to get her mind off the fate of the world. A little alone time with her man and a nice soft bed. Then they could get back to the fate of the world and their place in it.

The Masters' tribe would continue to thrive and Ive would do everything in her power to protect her new family.

"You ready for me, Ive." Dji had got close enough to whisper in her ear and followed it up by nibbling on her neck. He knew that was a total hot spot for her. God, she'd take him here and now if he didn't stop.

"I've been ready for you my whole life." Ive winked and opened their door. "Now show me what you've got."

She shut the door behind them and closed out the world — just for a little while.

ABSOLUTION

Dedication

This one is for me. Dreams, book one of the Seeds of Dawn series, was the first story I wrote for publication. It wasn't my first book published, but it was my first Total-e-Bound story in the anthology Over the Moon. Absolution is the last book in the series and it's hard to believe it's coming to an end. It's been a great ride with the Masters pack and I hope you've enjoyed your time with them as much as I have.

And thank you to Kelly who let me use her name. Hope you like your fictional character as well as your fictional partner.

Also a shout out to Kim, Jenn, Rhonda, Susan, Valerie and Jo for winning an auction and giving me the characters Peter and Everett.

Last but not least, Joy.

Prologue

"This is Jill Scott with the late-night edition of your local news." She held a hand up to her ear and looked confused before speaking again. "I'm getting some breaking news. My station manager has just informed me that the following video you are about to see is not a hoax. I repeat, this is not a hoax. Last night our camera crew caught something extraordinary on tape. The kind of thing you only see in the movies. Take a look."

The reporter faded away and on the screen was an image of a man changing into a wolf, but the reporter's shocked gasp was caught on the audio. She seemed to compose herself back into her on-air persona. Her tone nice and even – as if she hadn't seen a person changing into a wolf along with the rest of the nation.

"We are not sure who this is, but if you have any information, the local authorities would like you to contact them. Please, keep your distance. We don't know if it's dangerous."

* * * *

Bella Pouge sat bolt upright in bed and clutched a blanket. She gasped for air and willed herself to calm down.

"Bella, honey, what's wrong?" David Sanders, her mate, reached up to stroke her back.

"Sorry, didn't mean to wake you." She struggled to calm herself.

"Mmkay. You good?" David patted her hip.

She looked down at him, his eyes were still closed. Bella smiled. He was still half asleep and trying to comfort her. Bella rubbed her stomach and sighed.

"I had a dream," she admitted.

"A vision?" David sat up slowly and pulled her to his chest.

"I—oh, God, David, I hope not." She snuggled closer, letting him comfort her.

"What is it?"

"Werewolves are going to be exposed on the nightly news if we don't do something to stop it. That is, if I had a vision."

"The Ancients said it would happen." David sounded resigned.

"I know, I was just hoping this once they'd be wrong. Things have been so good lately. Must have been the calm before the storm. We have too much to lose to let this just happen, David. If that news story breaks before we have a handle on the situation, we could all be caged as lab experiments or die." Bella's hands shook as she rubbed her belly again.

David put his hand over hers. "Let's go find Russell."

Bella watched her lover get out of bed, and prayed to the Ancients that they could weather this storm as they had all the others before them.

"Please let this be the last trial so we can have peace in the Masters pack."

David reached to help Bella out of bed. "It has to be, we've already been through more than one pack should have to." He kissed her on the check.

"If it wasn't for some of that trouble we would have never met. The same goes for most of the mated pairs in the pack."

"This is true, I wouldn't change any of that for the world, but it's time. We were lured into a false sense of security. We knew something like this would happen. We should have taken care of it months ago, but I understand Russell's reluctance. Hell, I don't want to become a scientific experiment any more than the next guy."

"Don't even tease about that, David."

"Who's teasing?" David patted her on the butt.

Bella just shook her head, rolled her eyes and continued dressing.

"The pack is still at the pond at the party Russ and Vivian put on."

Bella had been tired and they'd called it an early night, retiring to their house behind the big pack compound. She looked around at what had become her home. She wasn't going to lose it without a fight. *Bring on the humans.* They wouldn't wreck what she'd built. Bella refused to lie down and take what might be dished out. The Masters pack would be victorious. After all, they'd survived a lot of trials in the previous few months. She absentmindedly rubbed her stomach again.

Chapter One

"Dance?"

A hand appeared in Kitty Kelley's line of sight. She flinched.

Damn it, I'm stronger than this.

She hated the fact that she was reduced to jerking away at the slightest movement. She was safe now.

Kitty had been too busy keeping an eye on her twin sisters, Bunny and Poppy. Her parents had been high on drugs when they named them all. Who in their right mind would name werewolves after animals that wolves would sooner eat than play with, and a flower?

Her sisters had gone to get some punch. This was the first time the three of them had joined the Masters pack for an event since they'd been rescued from the Tyler pack. One of the few lucky breaks they'd been given in their lives.

It had been the pack alpha, Russell Masters, who'd insisted they join the festivities. He'd been so good to them over the last few months that they couldn't refuse. It was thanks to him they had a roof over their heads and they weren't starving.

Kitty smoothed down the front of her skirt to calm herself and looked up to see who'd asked her to dance. He'd pulled his hand back when she'd had her kneejerk reaction.

"Sorry, I didn't mean to startle you." Everett Cord grinned down at her and shrugged. He put his hand in his pockets and rocked back on his heels.

Everett was very handsome with his spiked strawberry blond hair and dark green eyes. He had a very appealing dimple on his chin. For some reason she wanted to lick it. The thought came out of nowhere. She shook her head.

He'd been there the day she and the girls had been rescued. It was Everett who pulled her and her sisters out of the awful pack house they'd ended up in when their parents had died. Murder-suicide and she really didn't want to think about that. Not now and maybe never.

Everett was losing his smile and backing away—it was her fault for not speaking up and getting lost in her own thoughts. *Shoot.* She couldn't have that. She needed to thank him.

"Wait. Sorry." She glanced at Bunny and Poppy, who were talking to a few of the other pack members and they seemed good—safe. They didn't need her hovering over them. They were sixteen going on eighty and would be embarrassed if they knew she'd been keeping tabs.

Kitty took a deep breath. *It's okay to let go and have a little fun.* She didn't have to worry about her sisters as much now that they were here. The Masters pack accepted them as their own. They'd proved it time and time again over the past five months.

"I would love to dance."

One of her favourite songs just happened to be playing, *Cowboys and Angels*. Everett bowed low and held out his hand, wiggling his fingers this time.

Kitty smiled. It felt good. She didn't think she'd ever be happy again. She placed her hand in his and he tugged her off her seat and guided her towards the dance floor.

They were in the forest, in a big clearing behind the pack house. Someone had strung up white lights in the trees and they twinkled over the pond. It looked like the lights were dancing over the water. The pack had set up the refreshments in between some trees leaving a nice space for dancing. Other couples were out there, but Kitty didn't really know them. Well, except for Peter, Everett's cousin, and Peter's partner Grey.

The couple had stopped by the cottage that she shared with her sisters. She thought it might have been because Peter felt guilty. It was his dad's pack who'd taken advantage of her and the girls.

Enough. Fun, that's why I'm here.

They reached the clearing and Everett twirled her around and shuffled her across the makeshift dance floor. He wasn't really following the beat of the song, but two-stepping her around at a fast pace. Kitty hadn't had this much fun in — she couldn't remember when. She threw back her head and laughed when Everett dipped her at the end of the song, she lifted her leg high and her hair brushed the ground.

The next song began to play and it was more romantic than the first one. She recognised it from the movie 'Armageddon', Aerosmith's *I Don't Want to Miss a Thing*. Kitty thought they'd go and sit back down, but Everett pulled her close and they swayed back and forth—so different from the playfulness of the first dance. He nuzzled into her neck and she laid her head on his chest. His scent was overwhelming, it made her feel safe and he smelt like cinnamon.

Mate.

No. Kitty stiffened in his arms. *That couldn't be right.* They'd met before this. How would she not know? *No, no, no, no, no, no.* She couldn't have a mate. It was destructive. People died. Kitty jerked away and scrambled backwards. Everett looked confused, but she couldn't speak even if she wanted to, because the panic was building too fast. She couldn't breathe. She had to get out of there. She turned and ran smack dab into a person from her past that she never wanted to see again. She backpedalled away and almost fell flat on her ass. She started to shake—this could be very bad. How the hell had he found them?

But there he was, Langford Harrington, her parents' lawyer. Langford put his hands out to steady her and Everett growled behind her. Langford didn't pull away until she was steady on her feet.

"Kitty, I see you're well."

"How did you find us, Mr Harrington?" Kitty clutched at her throat with one hand and wrapped her other arm around herself as she moved, focusing on not hyperventilating.

"You didn't make it easy, but now this bit of rebellion is over. You're needed back home." Langford reached out for her again, but he hesitated before dropping his arm.

Bunny and Poppy surrounded her. She hadn't even heard them come to her aid. She didn't think he was afraid of her sisters.

"They are home, mister. I suggest you leave." Everett was at her back and that would explain Langford's not touching her.

Everett's warmth was reassuring. And he was right, this was home now. Not her parents' estate or the Tyler pack, but here among this wonderful group of wolves who treated them like their own.

"Do we have a problem here?" Russell broke into her musings.

Now the alpha was by her side. Never had she felt more like part of the pack than right then. Russ didn't even know Langford, but he was stepping up to make sure she was okay and that said a lot about the Masters pack.

"He can't make us, can he, Kit? I don't wanna go back," Bunny whispered, almost in tears.

Kitty took her hand and gave it a gentle squeeze. She held out her other hand for Poppy, making a united front.

"No, you, Kitty and Poppy are staying here," Everett answered for her.

It was all very nice, but this was her fight and she had to stand up for herself. They weren't going back into the world her parents came from. High society with all its backstabbing was not an environment that her sisters should be raised in. No amount of money in the world would make that right. Her mom and dad found out the hard way when Mom went crazy, killed Dad, then herself, leaving Kitty behind to take care of the twins.

The best thing she'd done was run when her uncle tried—she wasn't thinking about that. No. Everett gripped her shoulder and she calmed. She could do this.

"Like Everett said, we are home and have no intention of going with you. Good evening, Mr Harrington."

"Your Uncle Kurt isn't going to let this go, Kitty. Just come back and we can deal with the paperwork and get things transferred over to you. It's that simple." Langford was using his soothing lawyer voice, but it wouldn't work on her this time.

"Then we can do it here," Kitty insisted.

"I didn't bring the papers with me. We're talking about a lot of money here. Let's —"

"No. You can go get what you need and come back. We aren't going back to D.C. ever again." She was firm on that matter. It wasn't a good place for anyone. The city was toxic with all its politics.

"The scandal —" Mr Harrington began.

"I don't care about that." Kitty clenched her hands by her side.

And she didn't. So what if her parents' tragedy had been all over the news? So what if her dad had been some bigwig? That shouldn't matter to her and her sisters' wellbeing. They'd broken away and she wanted to keep it that way.

"You should." Mr Harrington moved closer, but stopped at Everett's growl.

If the situation wasn't so serious she might have smiled at Everett. She wondered if he knew they were mates because he was being very protective, above and beyond a pack mate, but she had to worry about that later.

"Leave." Kitty was proud of herself. Her voice didn't even break.

She released her sisters' hands and crossed her arms over her chest, her stance firm. She wouldn't budge on this issue. If she didn't have to leave the pack property she really didn't want to. At least not yet.

"You heard her. It's time for you to go. You can come back in the morning and we can sit down and chat, but now is not the time. As you can see we're in the middle of a party. And it's a bit late for a business call, wouldn't you agree?" Russell glared at Mr Harrington.

Finally the lawyer backed down, but he didn't cower under Russ' stare.

"As you wish, but this is far from over."

And it wouldn't be. Kitty knew that. Uncle Kurt would never stop until he had her back under his thumb and in control of the money their parents had left them. Not that she had any access to it, which was why they'd ended up in the Tyler pack to begin with.

Mr Harrington looked back over his shoulder, but kept on moving off the property, she hoped.

"Okay — let's get back to the party. Music?"

When had the music stopped? Kitty looked around and realised the whole pack lingered close by. She swallowed and took a deep breath. She couldn't cry right now.

"Russ!"

Kitty looked to the dishevelled woman running towards them. She couldn't remember her name, but she looked upset. Kitty began to back away, but Everett still stood behind her, foiling her escape.

"Bella, what is it?" Russ sounded concerned.

Kitty shouldn't be here, this had to be pack business, but she had nowhere to go.

"I had a vision."

Russ groaned and ran a hand through his hair. "Just when things settled down. I shouldn't be surprised. What was it about it?" He sounded resigned.

"It—Russ, it's bad. I saw a news broadcast where they caught a shifter in mid-shift. Humans are about to find out about us."

Kitty gasped and looked between Bella and Russ. The alpha had paled at the words and was incredibly still. Bella appeared to be shaking. This wasn't good. Bella bit her lip and her mate hugged her close.

Russ exhaled loudly, startling Kitty because he hadn't moved for what seemed like the longest time.

"Shit. We were warned this might happen. But we have the heads up now. We have to fix it—control the situation. It's destined to happen, but we'll break the news. I'm going to have to go visit the other packs and get them behind us before we go live."

"I can help."

Kitty looked to see who'd spoken up, but she was still bad with names. She must have looked confused because Everett whispered in her ear.

"That's Valerie."

Kitty nodded. The situation was fascinating, but— she stopped herself from saying what she was thinking. If she put it out there, she'd have to go forward and put herself on the line, and she had her sisters to think about.

"Valerie, that's a good call. You still have ties at your station?" Russ' shoulders didn't look as tense, and he was a bit more animated than before. That had to be a good sign. She wouldn't have to say anything. She could just go about her business.

"I do, but we're going to have to need something that gets the sympathy of the people." Valerie paced back and forth.

"I can help." Kitty slapped a hand over her mouth. *Why did I say that?*

Chapter Two

Everett looked at Kitty. God, she was gorgeous with her blue eyes and long blonde hair. And such a tiny little thing it looked like a strong wind would carry her away. She'd been so timid when they'd first met and he was proud of her for standing up to that lawyer. He really didn't think she would be able to. It looked like living with the pack had helped her find her courage. There was more spirit in her then he'd ever imagined and it made him hard. Wildly inappropriate, but what was a guy to do when his mate looked so fierce? And of course he'd been hard almost the whole time they'd danced. At first he didn't think she was going to accept him. When she'd flinched at his touch, she'd nearly broken his heart. There was no way he would ever hurt her, but Everett had to be sure they were mates. The second he'd pulled her close, he'd known it was more than just regular attraction.

Yeah, he figured she knew they were mates as well, after her mad dash away from the dance floor. He'd thought she might've been on that day he'd rescued her from his demented uncle, but didn't want to push it—at least not then. At that time he'd only wanted to get her out of a bad situation. He came to find out her sisters were younger than he'd first thought too. Good thing they'd got them out when they did. Who knew what kind of mental and physical damage could have been done to all of them?

Now Kitty was volunteering. How could she help when the news that shifters were real broke? If it was up to him she would stay far away from it, but it wouldn't be his decision. Hell, he wasn't even really part of her life yet. It would be up to the alpha to figure out how she could help, but she wouldn't be doing it alone. Everett would be there every step of the way.

Kitty looked horrified that she'd spoken up and her sisters appeared nervous. This didn't bode well. Everyone around them waited for her to say more and Everett knew she was about to bolt, he felt her tensing up. He gripped her shoulder and gave it a squeeze.

Poppy and Bunny huddled around Kitty. She pulled them close, but the deer-in-the-headlights look didn't go away.

"Kitty, how can you help us?" Russ' voice was all calm and authoritative.

"I...I..." She shook her head and pushed back against Everett.

"It's okay, you know you can—" Russ began.

"Hey—Russ, could we maybe...table this for now? It's not like it will happen tonight, right?" Everett glanced at Bella.

"Usually the Ancients give me time after a vision, but I never know how long. It could be tomorrow or a month from now. It's never cut and dry with them."

"Okay, do you remember which broadcast it was? Evening news? Morning?" Everett smoothed his hands down Kitty's arms.

Bella closed her eyes and it took a few moments before she spoke. "It was late night so that would mean — what? Ten o'clock news?"

"Good, that's good. Russ, can we do this in the morning?"

Everett's taking over didn't seem to faze Russ. If it were any other man, he'd probably have put Everett in his place, but Russ had a way of really listening to his people and that was what made him a great alpha.

"That's a good idea, Everett. It'll give me some time to do some brainstorming. And Kitty — you don't have to help, I'm not going to hold you to anything, but I'd like your input. We can all talk after breakfast in the morning." Russ nodded and left, but not before patting Everett on the back.

It was just him and the three sisters off to the side of the dance floor. "Why don't I walk you guys back to your house, unless you'd like to stay here at the party?"

Kitty turned to face him. "Thank you, for that. I — um — Yes. Please, I'm ready to call it a night. Girls?"

He liked that she included them and didn't force them. He wasn't surprised when they both nodded and started walking towards their cottage. Everett knew where it was, he'd helped them move in, not that they had much stuff. Grey and Russ had gone back to the Tyler pack to get what the girls had left there.

Speaking of Grey, he and Peter weren't far off and kept peering at him. He grinned and waved them off. He'd have to talk to them later, but for now he had to get the girls to the place where they felt the safest.

They would all be shaken up with the appearance of the dude Kitty had called Mr Harrington. It didn't look like they'd had much luck in the past if that lawyer was there on behalf of their dead parents. Kitty had looked scared before she'd taken charge.

Everett hoped he could get Kitty to talk to him before the guy showed back up at the pack house, but he didn't think there'd be time with the meeting after breakfast. If Everett had read the situation right, the lawyer would be back banging on the door first thing, but if the guy touched Kitty one more time, Everett would rip his face off. It was a close call tonight, but he'd managed to keep his wolf at bay. It wasn't like he and Kitty had bonded yet, they hadn't had any time. Well, he could have made time, but he wanted her to be secure in her place within the pack before he even looked into them being mates. And now—now he knew she was his.

Sometimes, being a wolf sucked with all the mate crap. He remembered how it had almost destroyed his cousin, Peter. Of course all of Peter's 'I'm gay and can't have a mate' thing hadn't helped the situation. But now he was happy with his mate, and someday Everett wanted that too. It hurt that he couldn't stay with Kitty, but it was too soon, if her earlier reaction was anything to go by. He'd just take her to the door and drop her off. It would take all of his willpower to back off. His wolf was pissed and wanted to break free, but Everett held himself in check.

They had a nice walk through the woods to get to Kitty's house. The pond area was secluded for trysts, more than one wolf got busy there. Maybe—yeah, he wouldn't think of that. No need to get hard and have his pheromones go all crazy. Not when the girls would have been able to smell him. Earlier it wasn't such a big issue because the clearing had been full of horny wolves. Here—with just the girls, talk about embarrassing.

Poppy and Bunny hurried inside, Kitty hovered at the door. "Thank you, again, for—you know—being there." She gave him a hesitant smile. She played with the knob and nibbled on her lip.

Everett traced her mouth with his thumb, getting her to release the poor abused flesh.

"Kitty—" He looked into her eyes.

"No, please don't. Not yet." She stood on her tiptoes and brushed her lips against his mouth before turning and going inside.

He stood for a few minutes looking at where a second ago Kitty had stood. He bowed his head and took a deep breath. His mate was on the other side of that door and there was nothing he could do about it. Everett wouldn't force the issue. It wasn't in his nature. There was always tomorrow. No matter if he wasn't in with the core group of the pack, he was going to be at that meeting.

The walk back to the group didn't make him any happier. He stood at the edge of the party. The dance from earlier still ran through his mind. They'd had fun. If that lawyer hadn't shown up maybe he could have calmed Kitty down enough to talk.

Peter must have seen him because he tugged Grey over to where Everett stood.

"Hey, cuz, what's up?" Peter stopped in front of him, blocking his view of the festivities.

The music was still country and the twang echoed around the clearing.

"Kitty's my mate." Everett blurted it out. *Shit*, he hadn't mean to do that, but he needed to tell someone and Kitty wasn't talking—yet.

"Okay, then why are you here?" Grey slapped him on the back.

"I—we…it isn't time. Not yet." Everett sighed.

"Ev—" Peter began.

"No, Pete, this isn't like with you. I'm not running, I promise, but she isn't ready yet."

"I wasn't ready either. I don't think most of us are, some less than others." Peter looked a bit ashamed.

Everett hated that look on his cousin's face. He had nothing to be ashamed of.

"I think we have more worries right now besides my mate. Did you guys hear Bella earlier?" Everett changed the subject because he didn't want to admit how right his cousin was.

"No, we were busy dancing." Grey winked at Peter.

Everett laughed. He liked how playful Grey could make Peter. And now he looked happy—no more pinched look, he was at ease and leant back so Grey could hold him. Everett didn't think he'd ever seen Peter so relaxed in his own skin. It had been a long time coming and he hated to take that away from him, but this had the potential to be bigger than anything.

"We're about to be exposed to the humans. Bella had a vision."

"Fuck," Grey whispered.

"Exactly. They're having a confab tomorrow morning so the pack can handle the news break. Things are about to get dicey real soon. Maybe you guys should—"

"Don't you finish that sentence, Ev. Don't you dare. We are pack and we won't go into hiding." Peter reached out to squeeze Everett's arm.

He should have known his cousin wouldn't just leave. The Masters pack was everything to all of them. They couldn't have a better leader than Russ and

Everett knew Russ would do whatever it took to protect everyone.

"You're right. I know it. I'm going back to the house to get some rest. I want to be there tomorrow. Kitty said she could help and I want to make sure if she does, she knows I have her back."

"We'll be there too." Peter nodded.

Everett smiled and nodded. It was nice having family to stand by you.

"Thanks, Pete." He turned and walked away.

Maybe he wouldn't go to bed just yet. He needed a run to wear himself out. He stripped out of his clothes and shoved them under a bush before shifting. He raced through the wood.

The trees were a blur. The small animals didn't tempt him. Usually bunnies were good for a hunt, but that only made him think about Kitty and her sisters. He was trying to get them off his mind so he could sleep. It wasn't working. Nothing was. All he wanted was to mate. His wolf agreed. Now wasn't the time. Everett had to keep that mantra going through his head. It was the only way he would not race to Kitty's place and lay claim to her.

He was panting by the time he got back to his clothes, and he couldn't run anymore. Everett lay down and collected himself before shifting back. He liked his wolf form, but everything was more primal. The run had done nothing to really clear his thoughts.

The shift back was fast. Everett tugged on his jeans and gathered the rest of his clothes before heading to his room in the big house. It was like a big dorm. All the single shifters lived there, leaving the houses for the mated pairs and the families.

It wasn't a bad place, but he missed Peter since he'd moved out to his own place. All of the smaller houses were being filled. A lot of pairs had got together in the last year. The pack was growing in leaps and bounds. Hell—they even brought one of those old shifter dudes back from Africa.

And now they were about to be exposed. It blew donkey balls.

Chapter Three

Kitty barely tasted breakfast. It was a nice meal of scrambled eggs, bacon and toast, all of her favourites, but all she could think about was afterwards when they would have the meeting and she'd have to reveal parts of her past that she really didn't want to. If Bella was right, their whole species would be in danger. She had no idea about the Ancients, her home pack had never talked much about them. They were never as spiritual as the Masters pack seemed to be. Kitty had missed all the drama over the past year or so. She felt bad for the Masters, but happy that her little family hadn't been there.

Now this.

"Kit, you okay?"

Kitty looked at Bunny. Her sister appeared nervous and Kitty couldn't have that.

"Yeah, you've been playing with the eggs. They're good, you should eat them." Poppy nudged her with an elbow.

"I'm good. Promise. Finish eating and you can go back to the house."

"What about you?" the twins said at the same time.

She had to grin, they were so in tune. Sometimes they even finished each other's sentences. It could be a bit creepy, but she was used to it.

"I have a meeting with Russ." Kitty pushed her eggs around her plate before she took a bite.

"Are we in trouble?" Bunny worried her lip.

"Trouble? No, honey, I just need to discuss a few things with them. That's all." She patted Bunny's leg.

"They won't make us go back, will they?" Now Poppy picked at her food.

"Nope. This is our home now." Kitty looked at them both, trying to reassure them any way she could.

"Good, I like it here." Bunny grinned.

"Me too, sweetie, me too. Now finish up. You two have chores."

"Aww...Kitty." They both groaned.

"Don't you 'aww, Kitty' me. If you want me to take you into town later for some shopping you'll clean up your rooms."

Not to mention she needed to look for a job. She'd managed to stuff some money away before they left, but a lot of that had gone to the Tyler pack. They were supposed to have helped Kitty get what was rightfully hers from her parents' estate, but that had never happened as far as she had been able to tell. Now Mr Harrington had shown up. She'd bet her last nickel that bastard Roger Tyler had told Mr Harrington where to find them. Roger hadn't been happy when they left. Well, he hadn't been pleased period with his gay son showing up. If they'd stayed after that, who knew what condition they would have been in. Roger had a heavy hand and he didn't care who he hurt.

"We're adults, you know. You don't have to baby us." Bunny pulled her out of her musings.

Teenagers. Kitty was just happy they'd started acting their age. For too long they'd been so quiet and almost perfect.

"Yes, I know, you're old enough to clean your rooms without me telling you. So…do it." Kitty laughed.

"Whatever." Poppy shoved her food into her mouth before getting up from the table.

"Dishes," Kitty reminded her.

Poppy grumbled, but did what she was told. Bunny did the same. Usually the housekeeper took care of those things at home, but things were different now.

Kitty glanced around and most of the pack had left. Russ and Vivian were at the head of the table, talking. Peter and Grey were still there, as well as Everett. She'd known he'd been there the whole time. It was like she had radar and it was tuned into the Everett station. He'd looked at her a few times—she could feel his gaze. And there it was again. She glanced up and away quickly.

Russ stood. "Let's adjourn to my office."

She gathered her stuff and left it in the kitchen. It wasn't her day to help in there. They had a schedule and rotated dishwashing and cooking. She was on tap next week. She liked the steadiness of it all.

Everett fell in to step beside her on the way to Russ' office. She glanced back to see Peter and Grey not far behind. Nobody spoke until they got into the office. Russ sat behind his desk and Vivian stood beside him.

"Okay, for those of you who don't know, our newest member is Kitty Kelley. Kitty, I'll introduce you to everyone. Over on the couch are Valerie and her mate Max, beside them is Joy and her mate Zareb. On the other side of the room are Bella and her mate David. You know Peter, Grey and Everett, right?"

Kitty nodded and looked at the floor. She hated the focus being on her.

Russ continued. "Last night Bella had a vision that we are about to be exposed. We have no idea when, but we need to assume it's soon. We're going to use Valerie's media connections to release our news."

"We need to find a sob story and get it out there. Something that will get the people on our side and if someone has any government contacts now would be the time to speak up. If we get an 'in' with them maybe they can help us." Valerie stood and paced the room.

It was time. She needed to speak up, but her family might make the situation worse. She cleared her throat.

"Kitty? Is this why you said you could help last night?" Russ' voice was low, as if he was trying to calm her.

"Yes," she whispered and cleared her throat again. "Yes. I'm the daughter of Arthur Kelley."

She waited for it to sink in. It didn't take long. Her family had been front page news for months.

"You mean—the Secretary of Defence? The guy whose wife shot him and then herself? *That* Arthur Kelley?" Valerie turned to look at her. Kitty nodded. "Well—fuck. That might not help us. It would show that we can be violent if they know your folks were wolves." Valerie began pacing again.

"I thought about that, but I can use contacts to let others in D.C. know. Some of them my father took into confidence so the knowledge that shifters exist is already out there. If we can get the President on our side it would help our cause."

"Good, that's good. We need some established couples to interview. That would help. We need some from the other packs as well." Valerie was almost talking to herself.

"I agree, which is why I called a meeting with all the alphas in the United States. After that we can contact alphas in other countries, but for now we all have to be on the same page."

"My dad—" Peter started, but the alpha didn't let him finish.

"I'm stronger than he is, Pete, he'll listen to me," Russ assured Peter.

"I think we need Bella and David as the first interview." Valerie turned to the couple.

David didn't look happy. Nobody did, not that Kitty blamed them. The situation was beyond crappy. It sucked that they would be exposed. They should've been able to stay in hiding. It wasn't like they were hurting anyone.

"What?" David stood and scowled.

"Dave…she's right." Bella stood and gripped David's arm.

"I don't want—" David turned to Bella.

"This isn't only about us and you know it. I'm pregnant and it shows. I'll be perfect." Bella stroked David's arm and it appeared as if it was calming him down.

"And you're both attractive and calm types. That'll help. I think Peter and Grey should—"

"Oh, hell no." This time it was Grey who stood.

The whole room was tense. Kitty hated it. She clenched her fists. Everett took her hand in his and laced their fingers together. It helped more than she was comfortable with, but he was her mate. They'd probably have to talk when all of this was over.

She was scared though, she didn't want to end up like her parents.

"You represent the foxes *and* you're a gay couple. We need to come at this from *all* sides." Valerie didn't look at any of them. She still appeared to be scheming.

There was a knock on the office door. Everyone turned and stared.

"Enter." Russ raised his voice.

Kitty figured it was so the person on the other side could hear, but she still jumped.

One of the pack members Kitty didn't know stuck her head in. "Russ — there's a Mr Harrington out front to see Kitty."

"Thanks, Erin. Give us a couple of minutes and I'll send someone out to get him."

Erin nodded and left, closing the door behind her.

"Okay, this is over for now. I have the other alphas due to arrive this afternoon. Valerie, get your contacts together and start on your interviews. I'll want to take a look at it before it goes live."

Valerie nodded and left the room, Max on her heels. Joy and Zareb were next, followed by Bella and David. Peter, Grey and Everett stayed in the room.

"I take it the three of you are staying?" Russ raised an eyebrow.

"Yes, Russ, we are." Everett spoke for all of them.

"Good. Kitty, do you know what Langford Harrington wants?" Russ tapped his fingers on his desk.

"My uncle Kurt wants me and my sisters under his thumb so he can take control of our inheritance."

"It's more than that, isn't it?" Russ looked right at her.

He must have smelt her unease. The small room didn't leave her anywhere to run.

"He...ahh...the reason we ran was because —"

"You're safe here, Kitty. Go ahead." Everett squeezed her hand.

"Uncle Kurt wants more than the money. He wants me." Kitty flashed a quick glance at Everett, then down at their joined hands.

Everett growled.

"Well, as long as you're happy here, you don't have to go back. Calm down, Ev." Russ smiled.

"But—he's my alpha." It was the first time she'd acknowledged that in a long time. He could call her back at anytime and that was probably why Langford had shown up.

"No, Kitty, I'm your alpha now." Russ stood and walked around his desk to stand in front of her.

"O—kay."

"And—you're my mate. He can't have you," Everett growled again.

"Plus, we have your back. You're family now, Kitty." Peter smiled at her.

Kitty gulped. She figured they could talk about that first, but it helped knowing the guys were on her side.

"Is this true?" Russ looked between the both of them.

"I—yes, sir. I just—last night—," Kitty began.

"I only confirmed it last night, Russ. We haven't had time to talk."

Russ looked over his shoulder. "Vivi, could you ask Mr Harrington to come in?"

"Of course." Vivian moved out of the room, but not before she kissed Russ' cheek.

"I know the two of you need to talk, and you can have that time, but we need to let Harrington know you aren't going anywhere and about the threat to the shifters. I couldn't get a hold of your uncle, maybe Harrington can. Would you be okay with that?"

"I have to be. This isn't just about me or my sisters anymore, Russ. It's about all of us. As long as he knows I'm off limits—I'll deal," Kitty assured him.

"Let's get this over with so you can contact who you need to. We need to get this ball rolling." The door opened and Vivian let Langford in before leaving.

"Mr Harrington, please have a seat." Russ gestured to the chair in front of his desk.

"I would like to talk to Kitty alone." Langford sat and put down a briefcase she hadn't noticed before.

"I don't think so." Russ moved behind his desk.

"This is a private, family matter." Langford didn't even fidget.

"We're family," Russ assured Langford. "Plus we have other business we need to discuss."

"Really? And what would that be?"

"Shifters are about to be exposed and I need to get all the alphas on board with a plan."

Chapter Four

Everett had no idea how Russ could be so calm. All Everett wanted to do was take Kitty out of the office and protect her, not sit there and listen to the douchebag lawyer try to talk his smarmy shit. Of course, Kitty wasn't Russ' mate so it was a bit different for the alpha.

"And you know this how?" Langford sounded so refined.

Kitty was totally out of Everett's league. She was highbrow society and he was a thug wolf who lived in the middle of nowhere. But he didn't care. The Ancients made them mates and who was he to fight that? He didn't want to. Everett had been lonely since Peter found Grey. He was man enough to admit it. Now the Ancients were giving him a chance and he was taking it.

"We have a seer in our pack. I was also informed many months ago that Everett and Kitty were instrumental in making things go smoothly when the time came to expose ourselves."

That was the first time Everett had heard that. Was Russ making it up? Kitty looked over at him and he shrugged. What else could he really do?

"Kitty is needed at home." Langford was firm on the matter.

Everett half expected Kitty to speak up, but she hadn't looked up from their hands since Langford walked into the room.

"Kurt might have informed you of that, but D.C. is no longer her home. Kitty has settled in nicely and has accepted me as her alpha, as is her right. She isn't being forced to stay here and if Kurt is any kind of alpha he wouldn't have let her stay in the Tyler pack as long as he did. He holds no claim."

"She is his blood, not just pack."

"Doesn't matter and you know it." Russ shrugged.

"I have paperwork for her," Langford insisted.

"Fine, you can have it brought here along with Kurt. I'm holding a meeting later today. If he can't get here in person then he can conference in. If that is all, I've got a lot of things I need to prepare." Russ dismissed Langford.

Everett wanted to grin, but stopped himself.

Langford stood and looked at Kitty, but Kitty didn't even glance at him. He stopped at the office door as if preparing to leave, but didn't seem happy.

"I'll contact Kurt, but he won't be happy about this."

"I don't know what to tell you, Langford, but there is nothing he can do."

"That's what you think. I've worked for the Kelley family for a long time. They have—"

"I'm sure he has contacts, but so do I. So tell him it's in his best interest to back off."

Langford nodded and left.

Nobody spoke for a few minutes.

"Everett and Kitty are important to this whole mess and we're just finding out about it now?" Peter was the first to speak up.

"Well, at the time, Kitty was new here and had been through an ordeal. Then—to be honest, I forgot about it. Things were calm. I figured the threat of exposure was over. I should have known better." Russ ran a hand over his face.

"I'm sorry," Kitty whispered.

"Hey—hey, no, none of this is your fault. It's fate or the Ancients. Some call it destiny." Everett pulled her close and hugged her tight.

"He's right, this would have happened if you were here or not. I'm thankful you are here, though. You have some D.C. contacts that I don't. We're going to need all the help we can get and fast. I hate to—"

"It's okay, Russ. I'll go and make those calls." Kitty flashed a small smile.

Everett could tell her heart wasn't in it. He wanted to go after her, but she was going to need some time to be with her sisters.

"I'll come by in a few?"

"Yes, I'd like that." Kitty's smile was more real that time.

She left the office and shut the door behind her.

"Russ—," he began.

"I know, Ev, I know. I should have said something, but things were good and I didn't want to mess with that."

"How are we the key here?"

"I have no idea. You know how mysterious the Ancients can be. Maybe it only has to do with the two of you getting together so Kitty can use her contacts to break the news about shifters. I hope that's all. Getting the packs together is a good thing even if the news doesn't break. There has been too much corruption, what with Vivian's den and Peter's dad. They need to be taken care of. But we can all hope this is the last trial we have to go through."

"How is Bella doing?" Peter asked. "She didn't have another dream, did she?"

"She hasn't said anything and you all know she would if she had something. She's driving David to distraction with all her cravings, but it'll be nice to have a few pups around. She and Erin should have babies around the same time. Just like the Ancients predicted. Of course now Zareb and Max are running scared because they're next in line for babies according to the prophecy."

That made Everett smile. He didn't know Zareb too well, but to picture Max as a daddy? That was enough to make anyone have a laugh.

"So we focus on taking control of our exposure then batten down the hatches and ride the wave until things calm down?" Everett asked.

"That about sums it up. Peter, Grey, get ready for Valerie to interview you."

Peter groaned.

"I know it isn't something you want to do, but Valerie *is* right, we need to hit this from all sides."

"I know, Russ. I don't like it, but we'll do it." Grey stood and held out his hand to help Peter up from the chair.

Everett moved to follow them.

"Ev, hold back for a minute?" Russ spoke up.

He nodded at the guys and sat back down.

"What did you need, Russ?" Everett was anxious to get to Kitty. He knew it hadn't been that long, but he wanted to see her.

"I want you to know, I'm not forcing anything. Kitty is safe here and I'd never—"

"I know, Russ. That's what makes you a great alpha. You have no worries from me."

"Good, good. Okay, get out of here and go talk to your mate. The others will be here in a few hours and I need to figure out what to say to them to get them on our side. Thank you, Everett."

He knew a dismissal when he heard one. He left the room and made a beeline for Kitty's house. He hesitated at the door. Maybe he should have waited. She was probably still on the phone talking to folks in D.C. They had time. Like Russ said, things didn't need to be rushed or forced, no matter what his wolf thought.

Everett heard footsteps coming towards the door. He knocked so they would know he was there. Bunny, or was it Poppy, opened the door.

"Hey—Everett, what're you doing here?"

"I need to see your sister." Everett rocked back on his heels.

"She's on the phone right now, but you can come in." She smiled at him.

"Ah—thanks—"

"It's Bunny."

"Sorry."

"No, it's okay, most people have a hard time telling us apart."

It really wasn't an excuse, he was a wolf. Their scents should differentiate them. He took a deep breath and again when Poppy walked in. Now he could tell them apart. It was a slight difference, but it was there.

"Everett, did Bunny let you know Kitty is on the phone? We were going to go shopping, but it looks like something came up. We're gonna just—yeah—come on, Bunny." Poppy took Bunny's arm and pulled her out of the doorway, slamming the door shut behind them.

No, they weren't subtle at all. Everett shook his head. What would it be like to be that young again?

"Bunny, Poppy, are you—"

Kitty entered the room and his body went on full alert.

"They left."

"Did they say where they were going?"

"No, just that shopping was cancelled."

"Shoot. I didn't want to, but I figured with the whole exposure thing happening I should get my contacts on line."

"Right, right. So, how did that go?" Everett put his hands in his pocket so he wouldn't grab Kitty and pull her close. God, he wanted to kiss her. To see what she tasted like, how she felt wrapped around his cock. Shit, he was getting hard. He closed his eyes and focused on keeping himself in check.

"I had to leave a few messages so now it's sit and wait. I want to be able to get Russ in to see the President. It's imperative that we have him on our side." Kitty backed away from him.

Not that Everett blamed her. He was pumping out pheromones like they were going out of style. He clenched his teeth and stood his ground, not getting any closer. He wanted her, but not when she was so unsure.

"We should talk," Everett finally said.

"About us being mates?"

"I think so. Yes. I want you really bad here, Kitty, but I'm willing to wait for as long as I have to."

"Really? You'd wait?" Kitty stopped moving and looked at him for the first time since she walked into the room.

Like he was just going to jump her. There was too much in her past for him to even think about it.

"Of course I would. You're in absolute control here. We're on your timetable. I know you have other things you need to deal with, I just want to let you know that I'm here for you and we can chat about whatever you want to — whenever you want to."

"You're not — upset?"

"Do I smell upset, Kitty? Calm down for a second." Everett still didn't move a muscle.

"It — I —"

"I know you sense how turned on I am. Go beyond that."

"No. You're...calm. There's no anger at all."

Everett smiled. "I want more than anything to get to know you. It's important, right? We need more, not just the mating bond."

"I don't know if I can be a mate." Kitty looked down again.

He closed his eyes and counted to ten before opening them. He didn't look at Kitty. Instead he looked around the room. It was a nice place, but not much in the way of personal touches. The walls were all beige with nothing hanging on them. The furniture was the stuff Russ had ordered in for them. He'd hoped that in all this time the girls would have made it feel more like home. It looked like they were just there for a brief stay.

"Kitty. Please, sit down. I'm not going to jump you, I promise."

"Okay."

Everett waited until she was settled, and took the chair that was to the side of the couch. He wanted to sit beside her. Not yet. He had to bide his time.

"Why do you think you can't be a mate?" He wanted to scream, *What the hell are you talking about?* He didn't want to corner her or she *would* bolt.

"Look what happened to my parents."

"I don't really hear about what happened to your parents. I don't think anyone really understands. The press doesn't always get things right."

"My mom, she shot my dad. Everything was fine. We were sitting down for dinner. And—"

"You don't have to tell me this, you know that, right?"

"I do. So you can understand. Let me—I have to get this out. I haven't told anyone everything. Not even the girls. They were staying the night with friends. It was just me, my mom and dad."

He didn't know if he was prepared for what she was about to reveal, but he'd said he'd be there for her and he would stick to that because no matter what, she was his mate and it wasn't like he'd get another one.

Chapter Five

Kitty couldn't believe she was about to spill everything to Everett, but he was her mate and he had to know why she was a bad choice.

"It was a nice night. Mom and Dad had been fighting about something for days. I have no idea what it was about, just that my mom was very upset. It was one of the reasons the girls left the house. They were tired of hearing it. So dinner was on the table and we were eating. All of the sudden my mom stands up and points a gun at Dad. I have no idea where it came from. It's like it just appeared in her hands. She screamed something, but I was frozen to my chair, mid-bite. I couldn't do anything. Dad stood up too and held out his hands. I think he was trying to calm her down or something. She wasn't having it at all. I flinched when she pulled the trigger.

"After the gun went off she looked down at it like she hadn't seen it before. Over and over she was screaming, 'What have I done?' I still couldn't move. I dropped my fork. The clatter was loud. I think it echoed in my head. I thought for sure I was next.

Mom looked over at me. She was struggling with the gun—almost like it was alive or something. She looked right at me and said—'I'm sorry, baby'. It was like the fight went out of her, she raised the gun, told me to look away and shot herself." Kitty sobbed.

She didn't remember Everett moving, but he held her and rocked her back and forth.

"Shh, Kitty, it's okay. I've got you."

"Don't you see—it could run in the family, she was crazy."

"Kitty, did you say she was struggling with the gun? Like she didn't want to do what she was doing?"

"I...I guess. Yes."

All she really wanted to do was forget that night. After it had happened she'd taken her sisters and run with them. She didn't get too far until the Tyler pack found her and all she wanted to do was stay away from Uncle Kurt. She would have done anything. It was one of her biggest mistakes, or so she'd thought. Now she wasn't too sure because it had brought her here, to the Masters.

"Think. Try to remember what they were arguing about."

"Ev—"

"Stay with me for a minute here. Think."

Kitty closed her eyes and replayed the event. It was difficult because of how long she'd been trying to suppress the memories. It was right there—Kurt, they were talking about—

"It was Uncle Kurt. They didn't like the way he'd been looking at me and Mom wanted him to stay away from the house, but Dad kept saying he was his brother and maybe she was imagining it. That night— that—at the table—"

Think...think...what did she yell?

"Yes, at the table…"

"She yelled at my dad. She said—she said, oh my God, Everett, she yelled, 'Kurt sends his regards'. Why didn't I remember that? That's a big deal, isn't it?" She looked over at Everett.

Why would she have blocked that bit of information? The horror of the whole thing was big, that was her only excuse.

"Yes, it is and once we prove to the world that shifters exist it isn't a big leap to magic and we can get proof that your mom didn't kill your dad. She wasn't crazy, Kitty, she was under a spell. We need to tell Russ before he meets with Kurt. Russ can't go into that blind, if Kurt has a magic user on his side who knows what else he could be capable of."

Kitty wrapped her arms around Everett and hugged him tight. She didn't want to let him go. Kitty nuzzled her face into his neck. His scent was overwhelming and it was like a weight had been lifted off her. Her mom hadn't killed her dad or herself. It had been her uncle. That bastard had taken her parents away from her and he was going to pay.

She licked his skin. It was salty and tangy all at the same time. Kitty did it again. Everett groaned and pulled her in tighter. It was okay to let go. Everett had her back, he was her mate. Everett took her face in his hands and she moved away from the yummy smell to look at him. His green eyes were so dark they were almost black. Kitty whimpered.

"Kitty—I—" He took her mouth in a kiss.

First he nibbled on her bottom lip before caressing it with his tongue. She opened to him, never before had she been kissed with such passion, it felt right. Kitty moved so she could straddle him. She rocked her body against his. They both needed to be naked. Now.

The front door slammed shut and Kitty jerked away. The girls. How could she forget they were here?

"You guys seriously need to get a room because—gross."

Kitty looked up to see Bunny hovering by the door while Poppy stood next to the couch with her arms crossed, looking disapproving, her nose wrinkled.

"Gross? Really? That's what you're going with? Come on, Poppy. Give them some privacy." Bunny moved farther into the room.

"Privacy? They're in the *living room*. And—he's a dude, of course it's gross."

"I think it was hot," Bunny defended them.

"You would." Poppy glared back at her sister.

Now the girls shoved each other. She should stop them, but it was kind of funny. Ever since Poppy had announced she liked girls the twins had arguments about what was hot and what wasn't.

"Just because I'm not a lesbian doesn't mean you can make fun. I think Everett is cute. But it's even better when Peter and Grey kiss." Bunny gave a dreamy sigh.

"That's just double gross."

Was Everett—? He was. Everett's face was turning red.

"Girls, don't you have something better to do?" Kitty broke in.

"No," they said together.

"We need to go talk to Russ anyways so behave or I'll be telling Peter and Grey you think they're hot." Kitty pointed at Bunny.

Bunny groaned and Poppy laughed.

"Don't think I don't know who you've been panting over, Poppy..."

"You wouldn't." Poppy looked horrified.

"You know I would." Kitty smirked at her sisters.

Everett chuckled, but hid it by pressing his face to her shoulder. She had thought last night at the dance was one of the best moments in a long time, but sitting in the living room with her mate and sisters — that topped just about any one memory she had. It helped that now she knew her parents had been murdered. The heaviness of thinking her mom had gone crazy had been bigger then she'd ever imagined.

"We just came in to tell you Joy and Valerie are going into town and said we could tag along if that was okay." Bunny looked at her hopefully.

She had to let them go sometime. They were sixteen and old enough to do more than she let them.

"That's fine. Just behave. You have money?"

Both girls nodded and rushed out the door as if she was going to stop them. Kitty shook her head.

"You guys should go on tour." Everett snorted.

Kitty smacked his arm and moved to get off his lap, but he pulled her back down.

"I like this." He nuzzled into her collar bone, peppering it with kisses.

"What? Watching me and the girls bicker?" Kitty closed her eyes and ran her fingers through Everett's hair.

"No, you — happy."

"I like me happy too. Now — oh, that's nice, but ahh — we should go. Russ. Yeah — Ev!"

He'd nipped where her neck and shoulder met.

"You're right. I don't want to let you go."

"The girls will be gone for a while. We can come back here after we're done."

"All right."

Everett let her get up this time. She held out her hand and helped him. She had to get her head back in the game. The information they had was important. Everett didn't let her go, he laced their fingers together, and they walked towards the big house.

"So, you've heard a bit about my family and you've met the girls. What's your story?"

It was a nice walk to the main house and she could use the time to get to know her mate.

"Well—you know my uncle Roger and what an ass he is. He's my mom's brother. She left when she met my dad James. He was part of the Masters pack and was visiting—I'm not sure why he needed to talk to my uncle's pack, but my mom fell in love and never looked back. Or maybe that should be they fell into 'mate' or 'lust'. But I try not to think about that—them being my parents and all." Everett winked.

"What's your mom's name? Are your folks still here?"

"My mom is Jerri. She and my dad are still around, but on vacation right now. They're on a cruise. They'll love you and the girls. I'll introduce you when they get back. You also know my cousin, Peter. He was kicked out of his pack and finally found his way here. It's been his home ever since. I have another cousin, Don, but you've met him too. I think he's been a bit brainwashed by his dad. If he could get away from Roger, he might be worth knowing."

"I agree with you there. He seemed okay unless his dad was there."

"I kind of figured. Nothing I can do about it now, right?"

"Right. I love it here with the Masters pack. Everyone is so welcoming. And it's nice to know that Poppy isn't the only gay person here. I worried about that. It wasn't that big of a deal at home, what with my dad being the alpha, but we kept it on the down low at the Tyler house because we'd heard the stories about Peter."

"How did you end up with Roger?"

"We were running. After my folks were gone my uncle...he...why is this so hard to say? He made a pass at me. Freaked me out and I just wanted out of there. Everything was all wrong. Don actually found us and welcomed us into the pack. We went, pack life is all we've ever known and I figured we'd be safe from Kurt. And we were, but not from Roger and all his anger."

"How long were you with them?"

"A month maybe. I kind of lost track of time."

* * * *

They finally reached the house. Everett opened the door for her, and they headed straight for Russ' office.

"I don't know if he'll be in here, but it's worth a shot. I know he had things to do to get ready before the other alphas arrived."

The door was closed. Everett knocked and Russ told them to enter. They stepped through. It was just Russ, thank goodness. She didn't know how many more people she could tell this story to.

Everett must have felt her hesitation because he squeezed her hand.

"What brings the two of you back?" Russ smiled at them and motioned to the chairs in front of his desk.

"I remembered something...it's probably important," Kitty started.

"Okay, what's that?"

"My mom—it wasn't her fault."

"The shooting?"

"Yes, the thing I remember…it was dinner time and it was only my folks and me. She stood up and shouted—'Kurt sends his regards' before she shot my dad. Then she struggled with the gun before giving up and shooting herself."

"Are you sure?" Russ' jaw was set and his knuckles white.

"Yes, sir. I wouldn't come to you if I wasn't. After my parents died, Kurt tried to get me to…he, ahh…that is…he wanted me for himself. I think he thought after my dad was gone, he'd be alpha and I'd fall in line, but I ran instead."

"And now he knows you're here. Things are never easy around here, are they? No worries, we'll figure this out. It means he has access to magic somehow. My pack has the only magical wolves that I know of. Do you know who in your pack might have helped him?"

"No, I don't. I wasn't aware of people who had magical powers until I got here."

"It could be those drugs, remember, Russ?" Everett broke in.

"Drugs?" Kitty was confused.

"There is a drug out there that can give shifters a magical boost. We ran into some of it not that long ago. It's a possibility. We need to get Zareb and Joy in on this."

"Will we be safe?" Kitty looked between the alpha and her mate.

"You have my word. I'll do everything in my power to keep you and your sisters safe."

Russ said it with such conviction she had no choice but to believe him. *Thank the fates that this pack found me when they did or who knows where I'd be.*

166

Chapter Six

Kurt Kelley paced his office waiting for the call from Langford. It had been too long already. The man should have got back to him by now. How was this difficult? All he wanted was Kitty. He had the pack, now he needed his mate and who better than the most beautiful wolf he'd ever seen? He'd been jealous of his brother when he'd married Ginger. He'd tried everything to get the woman to pick him, but she went on and on about how it wasn't true love for them and how Arthur was her true mate.

Bullshit. There was no such thing as true mates. It was a fairytale elders told to keep horny young wolves from humping each other every chance they got. Well, Ginger and Arthur were dead and Kitty would be his. He didn't care about the other brat kids. They could stay where they were.

He didn't want to chance another hit of the magic dust he'd bought off the black market. It'd drained him that last time.

Finally his cell phone rang. He looked at the number before answering.

"Tell me you found her."

"I did, sir. She is with the Masters pack and has pledged alliance to them. But that isn't all. Russell, the alpha, requested that you meet with him. He said if you can't get there physically a conference call would do, but that shifters are about to be exposed to the humans and everyone needed to be in the loop."

"Who cares about that? Like humans could prove it without catching a shifter. Big fucking deal."

"He said they have a seer and she had a vision of the news catching a shifter mid- change on film."

"It could still be called a hoax. I want to know why you didn't just grab Kitty and bring her to me."

"It doesn't work that way, Kurt. She's an adult. I can't force her to do anything she doesn't want to."

"Then you should have grabbed the brats. She would follow them anywhere. Wasn't I listed as their guardian?"

"You were, but Ginger and Arthur changed their wills recently. Remember? Kitty gets everything, including guardianship of her sisters. Legally there is nothing more I can do, but give Kitty the paperwork she needs to get everything transferred to her name."

"What about the pack?"

"Technically it would be hers too, but since you are the relative here at the time, temporary control of the pack is yours. If she wants to come back, it reverts to her."

"Fuck. And you couldn't tell me this sooner?"

"I tried, but you just wanted me to get to Kitty. So that's what I did. Are you coming here?"

"Yes, I'll get on the first flight." He hung up the phone, not waiting for Langford to say anything else.

He had plans to make. The magic worked better when he was close. It had been fun watching Ginger shoot Arthur. He wished she didn't have to kill herself, but it was for the better. He figured she'd rather be dead than in jail. So ultimately it was for her. Kitty had been totally freaked out, but it had been necessary. She wasn't supposed to have been there, but plans had changed and Kurt already had the magic in his system so it had been 'go' time.

Kurt had questioned her after the fact, but she'd still been in shock. He figured she had no idea what really happened. If she did, someone would've been after him by now. He was safe enough. Once he got her home, he'd keep her locked up if he had to. She'd be his one way or another.

Maybe he would need the twins for leverage. He just needed to convince Masters that Kitty was crazy. They'd be begging him to take her off their hands. Then things could get back to normal. The scandal was already dying down and Arthur had been big on keeping his kids out of the news. Most people only knew he had three kids and no one had ever seen them outside of photos.

It would be safe to make Kitty his. He might need her to change her name—maybe dye her hair, but those were little details he could take care of later. For now he had flight plans to make.

Kurt called his butler and told him to pack for an extended stay away. He was living in his brother's house, it was bigger than his own, and he'd fired all the staff and brought in his own. So confident of his success, he'd already put his home on the market. Nothing could touch him. Even if Kitty did remember, the only people who might care would be wolves, and they tended to stay in their own packs. They wouldn't mess with him and if they tried, well, he had more magic dust to take care of that.

The world was his and he was taking it with both hands. Nobody got anywhere if they didn't take what they wanted.

He shut down his computer and informed his secretary he'd be gone for a couple of days and to shift all his appointments to junior members of the team. Kurt didn't have anything pressing on his calendar so it was a good a time as any. That was the joy of being your own boss in one of the most prestigious law firms in town.

* * * *

It didn't take him long to organise a flight and be on his way. He'd get to see his obsession real soon. What he wanted, he got. It had been that way his whole life and it wasn't going to change now.

Kurt had Langford meet him at the airport.

"Did you let them know to be expecting me?"

"Yes, sir. Here, let me take that."

Kurt passed off his suitcase and followed Langford to the car. He should have sent someone who wasn't loyal to his brother, but figured Kitty would respond better to the man. Langford had been a friend of the family for a long time. Kurt might have to get rid of him at some point. Just fire him, unless Langford gave him grief.

"Are we headed straight there?" Kurt inquired as he got into the back seat of the car.

Langford glared at him, but Kurt ignored it. It was his due to be driven around. He didn't need to be in the front seat with a person who was beneath his social standing.

"Yes, the other alphas are there and they are waiting for you and one other to arrive so they can start the meeting."

"Good. Is it very far?" Kurt glanced out the window. He was bored, but he figured Langford needed the small talk.

"It's a good distance, yes. The Masters pack lives in a secluded area away from town."

That would work out perfectly. Now he just had to corner Kitty and get her to come home with him.

"Did you request an audience with Masters for after the meeting?"

"No, Mr Kelley, I didn't know you wanted me to."

"Of course I wanted you to. I need to talk to him about bringing Kitty back with me."

"Mr Kelley, I already—"

"I really don't care what you think on this matter. She may be an adult, but she is still a member of my pack."

"Technically, sir, it's her pack."

"Did you inform her of that?"

"Yes, I did as part of the legal paperwork I brought for her to sign."

"I thought she was signing it at home."

"That was the plan, sir, but she didn't want to go back to D.C. so I had to have the documents faxed in for her to look over before the courier got here with the originals."

"Have they been signed?"

"Yes. Well, the copies have, just to note that she's read them, but she'll have to still sign the originals as soon as they get here. They shouldn't be that far behind you."

That was it, Langford had to die. What an incompetent—he knew Kurt wanted Kitty back in

D.C. Kurt gritted his teeth. There would be time to deal with Langford later. For now he had to get through the stupid meeting and get Kitty alone long enough to work his mojo on her and get her home. Once she was under his thumb there would be no way out for her. If she was good, he might let her sisters come along, but if she gave him a hard time—he'd have them killed. Then she'd have nothing, only him.

"There's something else you should probably know."

Langford paused. This couldn't be good news.

"And…"

"She has a mate."

"What are you babbling about?"

A mate? She can't have found someone. Not yet. She was mine, damn it.

"A member of the Masters pack is her true mate."

"Bullshit."

"No, sir, it isn't. I met him and they are—"

"You will not finish that sentence, Langford, or I'll fire you on the spot."

He'd lost Ginger to his brother, he wasn't going to lose Kitty.

"Don't you want your niece to be happy?"

Langford wouldn't understand and it wasn't any of his business anyway.

"Just get me to the meeting."

****

About a half an hour or so later they pulled up to a house that was set back in the woods. It was a nice place. Much better than the pack house back in D.C. They had to drive for miles to find a decent place to shift. Masters didn't seem to have that problem.

They were escorted to an office. Langford remained outside.

"Hello, I'm Russell Masters."

"Delighted to meet you. I'm Kurt Kelley. I believe you know my nieces?"

Did Kurt see a tell-tale change in Masters' stance? It could be his imagination, but he'd be on the lookout for anything unusual.

"Ah, yes. Kitty, Poppy and Bunny are wonderful girls."

"Yes, they are, and I'd like to speak to you after the meeting, if you have a moment."

"Of course. If you'll have a seat, we're waiting on — ahh — there he is. Please close the door behind you, Don, and we'll get started.

"First, thank you all for coming on such short notice. My seer had a vision last night of a shifter mid-change on the news. Now — we could just gloss over it and keep living our lives, but the first place the newshounds are going to look is at the houses like ours with multiple people living in them. Or we could get the backing we need and let the humans know of our existence."

There was uproar as all the alphas spoke at once. Kurt was bored. He'd never be suspected so he really didn't care.

"Enough. Yes, I know this is a big step, but I'm not going into this lightly. The Ancients have said this will come to pass. The humans will know of our existence, the newscast is only the beginning. I don't want to be hunted down anymore than the next wolf. That is why I propose we stick together and break the news. I have a reporter here in the house who'll be doing a few human interest kind of pieces with a few of the mated pairs, so we are giving the humans faces to go with the fact that we turn furry every now and again."

A couple of the alphas chuckled. Kurt just wanted this meeting over with. He didn't care.

"Don, you're new to being an alpha, same with you, Kurt. Anything you'd like to add or share?"

"No, I think you have it covered." Kurt smiled.

"I'm backing whatever you'd like to do, Russ. I'm a bit uncomfortable with it, but my pack will deal."

What a suckup. Was the meeting over yet?

"Good. If any of you have members of your packs you think would be good for an interview, please let me know. Good candidates would be someone in high-powered jobs or just everyday kind of people. We have some spare beds for anyone who would like to stay and my door is always open for any questions."

"There is one thing," The Don kid spoke up.

How is someone so young in charge of a pack? He didn't seem very powerful to Kurt, but he'd always had difficulty telling who had the most juice pack wise.

"Yes?"

"I think we need an...I don't know, alpha's alpha. You have the most power and your pack is full of magic users. I don't know about the others, but we need to group together if we're going to get through this."

Now isn't that interesting? There are magic users on the premises. I'll have to be more careful.

"I'm good with that, if everyone else is. We should probably vote. If you do agree, nothing will really change, your packs would be your packs, but when it came to human relations, I'd be the go-to man for all of our packs."

A chorus of 'I agrees' came through. *What do I care?*

"Don—you could hold back a minute."

Well, shit. He needed to talk to Masters. It looked like he would be here for a while. But that was okay, he'd have time to go look for Kitty.

Chapter Seven

Everett knew Kitty's uncle would be showing up anytime and he had to take her mind off it. What better way to do that than dancing? They'd had fun last night—nothing said they couldn't again. The girls weren't due back for a bit. They'd called earlier. Joy and Valerie were going to get dinner in town so he and Kitty had the place to themselves. Not that they couldn't dance with the girls there, but he was hoping it might lead to more.

He was in luck. They had a small stereo in the corner of the room. He turned it on and found a station playing a slow dance. He didn't recognise the song, but it didn't matter, he just hoped they kept them coming.

Kitty came out into the living room and he held out a hand.

"May I have this dance?"

Kitty grinned and took the offering. Everett pulled her close and swayed to the music, nothing fancy, just holding her close was enough. God she smelt so good.

He nuzzled into her neck, never breaking stride. One slow song rolled into another.

"Kiss me, Ev."

How could he even think of denying her? He brushed his mouth against hers until she whimpered and opened up to him. He took the kiss as slowly as the dance — no need to rush, they had forever.

Kitty hopped up, and he had to grab her ass to keep from falling over. He backed towards the wall for more support. She made the most wonderful noises. Kitty moaned and her breath caught in her throat.

"You're driving me crazy, Kitty," Everett murmured against her lips.

God, he was shaking so hard, and he didn't want to drop her, and if she twitched just the right way he might've come in his pants. He hadn't even done that when he was younger. He needed to be inside her.

"Take me to my room, Ev."

That was music to his ears.

She looked into his eyes and he was lost. This was his mate asking for him. Some people never found their true mate. He was a lucky man and wouldn't deny her wishes.

"Where?" He didn't let go over her, just started walking.

"Down the hall, last door on the right." Kitty licked at his throat and nibbled on his ear. They stumbled, stopping along the way for a few kisses. He might have banged into the wall a couple of times.

How he managed to get to the room he would never know, but he got Kitty to the bed in one piece. He laid her down gently.

"Are you sure?" He had to ask because he didn't want to assume anything.

"Yes, I'm sure."

"I don't want to rush you, but my wolf — I might not be able to stop with just making love to you."

"I know. Mark me yours."

Now Everett was nervous, a shiver racked his body. It wasn't like this was his first time, but she was his mate, it had to be special. He moved off the bed and took off his clothes. He watched as Kitty knelt on the bed did the same. She was so gorgeous. Her skin was a golden colour and her blonde hair spread out around her on the mattress when she lay back down. Everett ran his hand down the middle of Kitty's body. She was so soft.

He didn't want to hurt her and if he didn't calm down he might. His shaft ached. All he wanted to do was fuck her hard, but not this time. This first time needed to mean something to both of them.

You only mated once and it was to be remembered.

Everett kissed any skin he could find, making his wolf calm down. He scraped his teeth over her nipples. She squirmed beneath him, causing the most luscious friction against his cock.

Mine, mine, mine.

His wolf was ready to mate. Ev took a deep breath. *Not yet.* Kitty ran her hands through his hair, petting him. It helped him to focus on her. The gesture was soothing. He moaned against her stomach before lapping at the sweet skin. He wasn't going to be able to hold back much longer. He was too ready to make Kitty his.

Everett hovered over her and licked at her throat before he bit down.

"You're mine, in mind."

Everett nibbled until he reached her chest and bit into the area above where her heart was. Kitty wiggled even more now and clutched at the blankets.

"You're mine, in heart."

He was getting choked up. These words were taught to all the kids as they grew older and the significance was always there. He moved his way farther down her body, tickling her stomach. He flicked her clit and fucked her with two fingers, then three to get her pussy ready. Not that she needed much, Kitty was so wet, God, he wanted to taste her, but that would have to come later. He had to finish the ritual.

Everett moved to where her leg met her pelvis and sank his teeth in before releasing her and saying, "You're mine, in body."

It was time. He sat back on his haunches and spread her legs wide before kneeling between them. He inched his dick inside, saying the words, "You are now mine, in mind, heart and body forever more."

A bright light filled the room, thunder crackled in the distance and everything was—more. He could almost taste the magic in the air. They were mates. Nothing but death could rip them apart. Kitty was his.

She clutched at his back and wrapped her legs around him.

"Ev—please—I need. Please—"

Everett rocked his body against hers. Kitty squeezed her pussy around his shaft. He wanted this moment to last forever, but if she kept doing that it would be over too soon. He took her hands and put them over her head, keeping his thrust slow and steady. Her breasts bounced with his every move, her nipples pebbled into tight pink nubs. Everett leant down and sucked one into his mouth, biting down and tugging.

"Ev—oh, oh…please." Kitty thrashed her head on the pillow.

He switched to the other nipple, giving it the same treatment. Kitty wriggled her fingers free and grabbed his head, bringing him up so he could kiss her. He devoured her mouth—thrusting faster and faster.

"Slow—Kitty."

"No—right there. Ev—I wanna, please, let me...oh God, Ev, Ev, Ev—"

She grabbed at his back again, clawing at him, egging him on. Everett lost his rhythm. He was going to come, but he wanted her there first. He plucked at her hard nubs before he ran his hands down her body. He gave her clit a hard pinch and she screamed, shuddering around his shaft.

That was it, he lost it. Everett threw his head back and howled, coming inside Kitty. He collapsed on top of her, but didn't stay for long. Everett rolled off and cuddled her to his side. Kitty stretched a leg over him and rested her head on his chest.

Neither said anything for a while—Everett basked in the glory of finally having a mate. They still had plenty to deal with, but their bond could only grow from here.

A door opened and closed.

"Shoot. The girls must be back." Kitty didn't even try to move.

Everett thought he should get up. He wasn't sure if they'd come into their sister's room or not. He didn't want to scar the girls for life.

"I should—"

"I don't want to move."

The bedroom door crept open. Everett reached for the covers and hurried under them, making sure they were both covered.

It wasn't her sisters. *What the fuck?* The man wore a suit and appeared dignified until he looked at Everett. A sneer appeared on his face.

"Girls—what are you…Kurt. How—why—?" Kitty scrambled to the headboard, taking the covers with her.

"Sir, you need to get out of this room now." Everett moved to get off the bed.

Everett didn't care who the guy was, but he didn't belong here. He wasn't expecting the growl. Kurt lunged across the room—his eyes wild and dangerous. Everett pushed Kitty out of the way and shoved at the running man. They both hit the floor with a thud. Everett was seconds away from shifting and bringing the crazed man down.

"Uncle Kurt, stop it right now!"

His mate had a powerful set of lungs on her, but it didn't stop her uncle. He was going to have to go wolf. He shifted into his wolf as fast as he could and charged, gripping Kurt's leg between his teeth. Everett shook his head and snarled, not letting go no matter how much Kurt struggled. Kitty called for him to stop, but he couldn't no matter how scared she sounded.

"Ev—please—stop, it's okay—let him go—Ev…"

Kurt had come into their space and attacked them. He had to protect his home, his family. Everett could feel Kurt starting to shift when he was jerked off him. He wheeled around to see Langford and Russ standing in the doorway. Kitty clutched a blanket to her with a trembling hand and she was very pale, her eyes wide. Everett shifted back and went for her, wrapping his arms around her.

"I'm sorry, Mr Masters, I was afraid something like this might happen."

"It isn't your fault, Mr Harrington. Please, call me Russ, and thank you for the heads-up."

Since when had Russ and the lawyer become buddy-buddy? Not that he really cared, he was actually thankful because if they hadn't stepped in he might have killed Kurt.

"You're welcome. And it's Langford. Kitty, if you're not going home, you need to name a successor."

"I agree. Kurt cannot be in charge of the pack. I think you're next in line. You can hold the pack together until my sisters are old enough to decide if they want to run it." Kitty didn't look directly at Kurt.

"I'm right here and you can't fucking do this to me. I'm the alpha. I'm in charge and you are mine."

"You're sick, Uncle Kurt, and you need help. I know it was you who killed my parents."

Langford's gasp stopped Kitty. God, Everett was so proud of his mate. He could see her running a pack, but he was happy she wanted to stay with him. Not that he wouldn't pick his life up and move with her. All she had to do was ask and he'd be there. That was what family was all about.

"Yes, Langford, you heard me right. Somehow he used magic to force my mom into shooting Dad, then taking her own life."

"I knew he was sick with his unhealthy obsession over you, but I didn't think he'd go this far. What can we do?" Langford adjusted his tie. That was the only outward action that Everett saw that would make him think the lawyer was unnerved. Langford still seemed so put together, as if they were in a boardroom or something.

"Not much. We need to keep him under wraps while we deal with the human issues. Russ, do you have a place here or should he go back to D.C.?" Kitty looked over to where Russ had Kurt by the scruff of his neck.

She was magnificent and he was getting hard. *Damn it*. Russ smirked at him. Everett flipped him the bird.

"It's probably best if he stays here. I can get Zareb to contain him so he can't mess with our big reveal."

"This isn't over, you know. I always get what I want," Kurt whined.

It was pretty pathetic, but Everett shouldn't have expected more from a man who had to have someone help him with his dirty work.

"That may have been the case in the past, but that is over. You killed my parents and that was your first mistake. Coming after me was your second. I'm not the same scared little girl. I've learned a few things. I'm strong and now—now I have a mate."

"No!" Kurt lunged for her, but didn't get far. Russ held him up short.

"Yes, Ev and I just finished the ritual."

"Congratulations." Russ bowed his head to them.

Nothing could ruin the happiness that Everett was feeling. He had his mate. Kurt wasn't going to be a problem anymore.

"Hey, what's going on?"

That slight bit of distraction was all Kurt needed to make his move. It happened in slow motion, or it seemed. Everett watched Kurt wrench out of Russ' grasp and charge Kitty. Someone screamed, it could have been him. He didn't know and didn't care. Everett scrambled to get to Kitty before Kurt could, but he knew he was going to be too late. She was too far away. Even if he shifted he wouldn't reach her in time. He tripped over the rug and sprawled on the floor. Russ was right behind him and jumped over him. Their main focus was getting to Kitty before Kurt did something that couldn't be fixed. Everett scrambled up, finding a bit of traction from the rug, but it wasn't needed. Kitty hauled back and slugged

Kurt right in the face. He went down clutching his nose.

Kitty shook her hand. "Ouch, ouch, ouch. That hurt."

"Are you okay?" Everett finally reached her.

"I hurt my hand."

"Well, it looks like you might have broken his nose so maybe it was worth it."

"It was. If you know what's good for you, Kurt, you'll stay down." Kitty frowned at her uncle, hands on her hips. Everett wondered if she realised she was naked, but he wasn't going to break the moment. She was an Amazon.

"I'd listen to her pal, if you don't—I'll let her loose on your ass. Got it?" Everett added his own glare.

"I think we've all had enough excitement for one night." Russ picked Kurt up and dragged him out of the bedroom.

"We always miss all the fun." Bunny pouted and Poppy nodded right alongside her.

Where did they come from? Everett was very aware of how naked he was. He reached behind him to grab a blanket or something, but Kitty thrust his jeans at him. He turned his back and put them on. Most wolves weren't shy about being naked in front of each other, but they were Kitty's sisters and young and—yeah, he'd rather have clothes on when dealing with them.

Russ, Langford and Kurt left the house. At least they wouldn't have to worry about the unknown that was Kurt. He'd be dealt with for killing Kitty's parents and that was the important thing.

"So, what did we miss?" Bunny winked at Everett.

Chapter Eight

Kitty yawned and stretched. It was a new day. She could almost believe last night hadn't happened, but she didn't want to wish it all away. Parts of it were good.

"Mornin'."

And that was one of them. Everett hadn't left last night. After they'd filled the girls in on what had happened Kitty had fixed them both dinner. The girls had their own things to do. Most of it had involved putting away the stuff they'd bought.

Kitty was just happy she didn't have to worry about supporting them. Their parents had set up a trust for Poppy and Bunny. No one would want for anything. Not that they needed much. Just each other.

And maybe Everett. Okay, most certainly Everett.

"Good morning." Kitty snuggled into his side.

Everett kissed the top of her head. "What's the plan for today?"

"Well, I need to call back the Senator I left a message for yesterday as well as the First Lady's secretary."

"You have the First Lady's phone number?"

"I met her one on one — once — and we've socialised a bit at different political events. My dad didn't introduce us to many people because he wanted his politics and his personal life separate, but I wanted to meet her so he made it happen. I'm hoping she can get Russ in to see the President so he can plead our case and get government support. I also need to let Russ know it's okay if he tells the President I'm a shifter. His wife can vouch for me — kind of — and so can the Senator."

"You really are the key to everything."

"Only your heart."

"You've got that right."

"Are you two done being mushy? I'm hungry," Poppy interrupted them.

Kitty had to look to make sure the door was closed.

"Your arms and legs aren't broken — make yourself something or see if they're still serving at the big house."

"Stupid guy comes in and…" her voice trailed off as she left Kitty's bedroom door.

At least she hadn't tried to open it. They'd have to set some new rules if — well — she should probably ask him.

"And ignore my sister. You could…I don't know…move in today?"

Everett tackled her to the bed and straddled her lap. "Really? Are you sure? It's not too soon?"

He seemed just as nervous about it as she was, that calmed her down.

"We're mated, Ev, of course I'm sure."

Everett leant down and nuzzled her neck, licking at the spot he'd bitten yesterday.

She shoved him off and put on some clothes before going to the bathroom. She wanted to kiss him, but not with morning breath. *Yuck.*

"Where are you going?" Everett struggled into his jeans and followed her.

"I need to brush my teeth so I can kiss you."

Everett grabbed her arm and tugged her to him.

"Kiss me."

"But—"

"Kiss me," Everett demanded again.

Kitty sighed, but reached up—getting on her tiptoes—and kissed him. It must not have been enough because Everett deepened the kiss. She moaned into his mouth.

"How romantic." Bunny's sigh had Kitty backing away.

She'd have to remember she had impressionable teens in the house, well, at least one.

"I thought you'd gone to breakfast with Poppy?"

"Not yet. You two are so dreamy together."

Everett was behind her with his head buried in her back. He shook and she figured that meant he was laughing. At least things wouldn't be dull.

"Ev is going to move in today."

"Cool. See you later." Bunny waved over her shoulder and left the house.

"You could stop laughing any time."

"No, I don't think I can."

Kitty shook her head. *Nope, never dull.*

"Do you want breakfast or not?"

"Yes, please."

"Good, now let me go brush my teeth."

"Yes, ma'am."

"Oh, I could get used to that." Kitty smiled at Everett and patted him on the cheek.

He had a strange gleam in his eyes. She figured now might be a good time to run. She turned and dashed down the hallway with Everett right on her heels. She let him catch her once they got into the restroom.

"We could take a shower." Everett had her backed against a wall, her hands by her head, and she couldn't move.

His body pressed against hers and she felt his arousal through his jeans. She wanted him again. As a matter of fact, she didn't think there would ever be a time when she didn't want him.

"Yeah—or you could fuck me against this here wall first."

Everett moaned, scraped his teeth down her throat and bit down on her nipple through her shirt. Kitty arched her back.

"Mine."

"Yes, I'm yours and you're mine," Kitty agreed.

"Against the wall, huh?" Everett winked at her.

"Think you're strong enough?"

Everett snorted at her challenge. He held both her wrists in one hand and reached between them to unbuckle his pants. He wiggled out of them until he was completely naked. She still had on a pair of sleep shorts and a T-shirt. Kitty wondered how he planned on keeping her pinned and undressing her at the same time. He pushed her shorts down and she stepped out of them. The ripping sound was her first clue as to how he was getting her out of her shirt. She looked down to see Everett using his teeth to tug on the material. It was one of the hottest things she'd ever seen. He finally let go of her wrists, but she was pressed tight against the wall. Kitty wasn't going anywhere and that was fine by her.

"Ev—"

"Don't Ev me now. You wanted it against the wall and challenged me. Against the wall it is. Can you handle it?"

"Yes, please."

He had the shirt open, but didn't bother removing it. She wrapped her legs around him and he cupped her ass.

"It's going to be fast and hard," Everett whispered in her ear.

"Oh—God, please." Kitty closed her eyes and leaned her head back.

His ripping her clothes off her was more exciting than anything she could have ever imagined. She was already wet and ready for him. All she wanted was him inside her.

Everett eased into her body. It was too slow after his promise of fast and hard, but he wouldn't let her hurry the moment. He pulled out of her just as slowly.

"Ev—"

He took her breath away when he slammed into her body. Over and over. This was what she wanted. Kitty had to hold on and enjoy the ride, her body slapping against the wall as she tried to meet his thrusts. It was wild, something so primitive, Kitty had never experienced such a connection before. It had to be the mate bond. She could almost feel Everett's passion as he pounded away. She was going to be sore, but she didn't care, it was worth it. Everett hadn't been kidding about fast and hard. Kitty was already on the edge. The force of his dick was delicious.

"Please, please, please." Kitty had no idea what she was begging for, but hoped Everett would give it to her.

And he did. Kitty bit down hard where his shoulder met his neck. Everett threw his head back and screamed her name. She scratched her nails down his back and squeezed his cock, massaging it with her pussy.

"Kitty. Close. Fuck."

"Come for me, Ev," she whispered against his ear.

His body stiffened and his movements became frantic. His chest hair brushing against her sensitive nipples pushed her over the edge.

Everett let go of her ass. She let her legs slide down, but he stayed pressed against her body. Probably a good thing or she would have fallen right to the floor. They both struggled for breath.

"That was—" Everett started.

"Spectacular," Kitty finished.

Her stomach grumbled. Everett laughed.

"Okay—shower and food." He put a hand on her stomach and moved from the wall.

It was comforting that he saw to it she didn't stumble. One more reason she was falling for him—hard. Everett turned on the water and got into the shower, motioning for her to follow.

The water was warm and the bathroom steamy. Kitty grabbed the soap to lather up her hands. She was going to touch Everett all over. She turned to look at him. He was so handsome and all hers. Kitty ran her hands down his chest, taking her time washing all his parts, paying special attention to his lovely, thick, veiny shaft. She tightened her grip and stroked Ev's dick. She couldn't believe he got hard again. Kitty wanted to suck his cock, to take him so deep he begged for mercy. Who was she kidding? She wanted it inside her again and again and again. If she had her way they'd stay in bed all day, but there were things to do, like stop shifters from becoming science experiments.

"What's wrong?"

She looked up at Ev. She'd stopped soaping him up, his hands held hers.

"Sorry. Nothing. I'm just thinking of what could go wrong."

Ev pulled her close and hugged her tight. "We can't worry about what might happen. We'll deal with what *is* happening." He kissed her forehead, took the soap from her and calmed her with his touch. He made quick work of washing them and rinsing off, but she wasn't done with him yet.

Kitty knelt in front of him. She wanted a taste and she was going to have it. Ev wasn't hard anymore and it was easy to fit him in her mouth. She could feel him growing, it was a fascinating sensation. Kitty swallowed around his dick.

"Kitty..." Ev ran his fingers through her wet hair. The water was warm against her back. She closed her eyes and sucked his cock, teasing the tip before deepthroating him. Kitty stroked his balls. They felt hot and tight, as if he was ready to come again. He thrust against her face and she squeezed his hips, letting him know he could take what he wanted.

He was nice and thick and Kitty had trouble getting him all down, but she used her hands to make up for it. Faster and faster until he shuddered under her. There wasn't much cum, but enough that she could taste his salty goodness. They'd have to do it again when he hadn't just had sex.

Everett looked down at her, tightening his hands in her hair as his shaft slipped from her mouth. "Thank you."

Kitty just smiled.

Ev helped Kitty to stand so she could step out of the shower and grab a towel. Ev didn't give her a chance to dry herself off. He took the big fluffy towel and stroked every part of her. It might have been a turn-on, but right then, it was more about comfort. As if he understood that she was a bit freaked and needed time. She closed her eyes and let him finish.

"Thank you." It was Kitty's turn to be thankful.

"My pleasure. Now, food before your stomach hurts us both."

And just like that, the mood changed again. He was everything she never knew she needed. Kitty wrapped her towel around her and picked up their clothes. They should have taken something in with them to change into, but they'd been busy with—other things. She had no idea when the girls would be back, but with her luck it would be any minute.

She passed Ev's clothes to him. He didn't have anything to change into—at least not until they moved him in. Kitty smiled. In this moment, everything was perfect. It might not last, but it didn't matter. They would always have this second in time that was theirs alone. No one could take that from them.

It didn't take long for them to get dressed. She was hungry so she didn't dawdle.

Kitty thought back to her parents as she headed to the kitchen and allowed herself to hurt for them, but she couldn't grieve yet. She wasn't ready. The reality that her mom hadn't gone crazy would eventually sink in, but she could deal with that later.

"I don't have much here. We usually head up to the pack house to eat. I think I have some eggs, maybe. I know I have some bread." Kitty headed to the cupboards and looked around.

"Kitty." Ev gripped her shoulders and rubbed them. "Talk to me."

He must have sensed her unease. Kitty laid her head against his chest, taking the comfort he offered.

"I...it's just...my parents."

"Ahh, it's sinking in that they were murdered." Ev hugged her. "It's okay, you know. You're allowed to be angry and upset."

"I can't." Kitty turned in his arms and pressed her face to his chest.

"Kitty—"

"Later," she murmured against him before looking up. "We have to fix this first. Then...then I can grieve. But now, let's eat." Kitty gave Ev a weak smile.

Ev kissed the top of her head and released her. "Okay, I'll check the fridge."

He released her and she watched him walk away. Every part of the situation was homey. Kitty had never thought of herself as domesticated, but it was— nice. Better than nice, it was actually kind of wonderful.

It made her remember her parents with happier thoughts. Her mom and dad had always had a great relationship, which was why it had been so hard to believe her mom could kill her dad. Kurt had taken that away from her, but she wasn't going to be a victim. Once shifters came out they could find a good punishment for her uncle.

Ev held up the eggs and cheese and wiggled them before coming back to the counter. This she could get used to, making breakfast for the two of them. The girls wouldn't be around for much longer, not if they were going to go to college, and if she had anything to say about it, they would. It was nice to know she wouldn't be alone.

Chapter Nine

Everett whistled on the way to the pack house. The sun was shining and all was right with his world. Breakfast had started off rocky, but after the food was done they'd talked about anything and everything — the kind of stuff that might have been learnt through dating. That was one of the great things about mates, usually they were very compatible. It might not be instant love, but that would come. He could see himself easily falling for Kitty. He had a mate and he was going to move in with her.

He opened the back door and ran into Peter. Literally. His cousin looked upset.

"Hey. What's up?"

"Don's here." Peter hugged himself, rubbing his arms as if he was cold.

"Where's Grey?"

"He went into town with Joy and Valerie. They made Ive tag along and Grey wanted to spend a bit of time with his sister."

"So — why is Don here?" Everett looked around like he expected Don to jump out at him.

"Stop doing that!"

"What?"

"You're freaking me out looking all around. He isn't on the first floor, at least he wasn't. He's staying in one of the guest rooms. He's the new alpha."

"Your dad?" Everett frowned.

"Forced to step down by Don. I guess things got worse. Mom was in the hospital for a while and Don woke up from whatever spell Dad had him under and realised things were wrong. I think, but I don't trust him. God, Ev, he—the things he did to look good to Dad—how do I forget that?"

"You don't." Ev pulled Peter to him, it was a bit awkward because Peter was a bit of a giant and Ev barely reached his neck, but that didn't stop him from comforting one of the most important people in his life.

"I need to get out of here."

"Go for a run and if you want, you can stop by Kitty's place. I'm moving my stuff over in a bit."

Everett hoped the run would distract Peter and give him time to find out what in the hell was going on. Last time they'd seen Don he'd been nothing but a shadow following his dad around and doing whatever he said. Poor Peter had taken the brunt of that when he'd come out. That wasn't how family was supposed to be. Thank God Peter had found him. It hurt Everett to think of the things his cousin had to endure.

"That's a good idea. Yeah, I'll go see your mate."

"Great. I'll see you over there." Everett gave Peter one last squeeze before moving around him and into the house.

He would find Don. *This had better not be some trick. If those assholes thought they could hurt my family, they are sadly mistaken.* A coughing sound made him pause on his way up the stairs. Don stood in the hallway looking uncertain.

I can stay calm and talk to Don or I can blow my shit and beat it out of the fucker. Everett closed his eyes and took a deep breath. He was above petty shit. He could be a grownup about this.

"I'm sorry."

Everett opened his eyes. He had to be dreaming.

"What?" Everett had to have heard Don wrong.

"I'm sorry," Don whispered.

"Why are you apologising to me?"

"Because Peter isn't going to let me and...I just—" Don began pacing.

"Why should he? You beat the shit out of him." And that was putting it nicely. From what Peter had told him it took him a month to fully recover and that was a long time for a shifter. He had been left for dead by his own family.

"Things are different now." Don stopped and stood in front of Everett.

He looked so pathetic with his sad eyes and his hair standing on end like he'd been running his hands through it for a long time. Everett didn't want to feel sorry for the bastard.

"Because Daddy isn't around anymore?" Everett shouldn't have egged him on, but he couldn't seem to help himself. The man in front of him didn't have the attitude of the man Everett had seen those many months ago when he saved Kitty from that awful pack.

"No, I found my mate."

"And she knocked some sense into you."

"He." Don said it under his breath.

"Excuse me?" Everett had to be dreaming. No way had Don just said he had a male mate, not after the grief he and his dad had given Peter when he'd told them he was gay.

"You heard right. 'He'. His name is Lincoln. Shit, Ev, I was young and didn't know any better and so jealous of my little brother for having the balls to come out. You know how Dad was, if he knew both his boys were fags—"

"Don't—," he began.

Don held up his hands. "Sorry. Just…this is hard, Ev. You were gone and Dad went a bit crazy. I did the only thing I could—self-preservation. Was it the right thing? Hell no. I know that now. I knew it years ago, but by that time it was already too late. I couldn't leave Mom and I had all of this misplaced anger building inside me, but then he went too far. They were fighting again, Mom and Dad, that is. He took her finger, looked her in the eye and bent it back, breaking it. He started hitting her and it was hard to get him off. I tried. It took five of us to restrain him. I…shit…I had to put him down. Do you know how fucking hard it is to…he was still my dad. Now—"

A short, dark-haired man came to stand beside Don and took him in his arms. The pair looked good together—like they belonged.

"Don, baby, you okay?"

"I'm good, Linc. I—"

Just like that, Everett had changed his opinion. Don was not the same person. Now he looked like the boy Everett remembered from when they were kids.

"Look, I can't guarantee that Peter will come around. There is too much shit there. But I can talk to him. It might be good for him to see the two of you together, but he might blow a gasket when he finds out you're gay, Don. I would expect a nice punch to the face."

Lincoln growled. Everett just smiled. He would've done the same thing.

"Don't go biting my head off there, Killer." Everett winked at Lincoln. "There's a lot of history that you —"

"Don told me."

"Then you know that it won't be easy for Peter. You need to give him some time. Make sure his mate is with him when you talk. That'd be your best bet. Now that we have that settled I have to get my shit moved out."

"What! You can't leave Pete. You —"

"Brotherly concern? How touching," Peter sneered.

Everett turned. He hadn't heard Peter come back into the house. Everett stood between the brothers. They weren't going to have a throwdown in the pack hallway.

"Peter —," Don began.

"No. You don't get to take that tone with me," Peter growled. "And what — you need a bodyguard now?"

This is going to get ugly. Please don't say it, Don. Don't do it...don't...

He tensed, waiting for the fallout.

"No. Peter, this is Lincoln Black. My mate."

Lincoln, the poor dense man, held out his hand like they were all 'happy, happy, joy, joy' with each other. Peter knocked it away. Lincoln was so short he made Peter look like a giant. No way was he dealing with this alone. He was the only thing between Peter and Don.

"Russ!" He didn't look away from Peter. "Peter, buddy, you need to calm the fuck down, right now."

"Ev, he can't — why is he — ?"

"We'll figure it out, but a fight here, it isn't a great idea."

Peter moved to get around him, then took a swing. Everett was able to duck, but the fist grazed Don's shoulder. Lincoln pulled Don back and growled. Don just looked so sad. Damn him. He was on Peter's side in this. Don deserved what he got. Peter charged again and Everett wasn't going to be able to stop him for much longer. He tried to get Peter's attention, then Peter went still. Everett couldn't explain the defeated look that crossed Peter's face. Lincoln held Don up, but Don wasn't fighting. He would have sat there and let Peter pummel him.

What a fucked-up mess.

Everett hadn't expected Peter to fall to the ground. Don finally had some life in him and moved in. Everett shook his head. Now wasn't the time for the brothers to be all buddy-buddy. Peter was going to need more time to comprehend what had just happened. *Fuck.* He wished Grey was there. He would've known what to do. All he wanted was get Peter out of there. Somewhere he'd feel safe. He had no idea why Peter hadn't gone to see Kitty, but maybe, just maybe the confrontation was good for him. Or it would be. Peter never had the chance to stand up to his brother before.

"Everett. What's going on?"

Finally the alpha showed up after all the action was over. Not a few minutes ago when Peter was going all mad dog on him.

"Don here was just telling our boy Pete about his mate. His—male mate, Lincoln." Everett waved over to where the two stood. It looked like Lincoln was holding Don back.

"I see. And where is Grey?" Russ crouched down beside Peter who was now clinging to his knees and rocking himself back and forth.

"He went into town." Everett knelt down at Peter's other side.

"We need to get him out of here." Russ looked at Everett.

Everett hadn't seen this side of Peter in a long time and he hated that it was back. He never wanted to see it again.

"I'll take him to Kitty's. It's far enough away. Send Grey over when he gets back, if you see him. And—could I get someone to pack up my shit and get it to Kitty's? I was going to move in today. If not, no big, I can do it later. Peter is more important."

"I'll get one of the guys to do it. You make sure Peter is all good." Russ stood.

"Please—" Don moved closer, dragging Lincoln behind him.

"Not right now, Don. You need to let him do this in his own time. Don't push him. Do you understand?" Russ used his alpha voice—the one that made Everett want to roll over and show his belly.

"I understand."

"It might be never. You've got to be okay with that. Maybe, after some time he can come to you. You'll be busy with getting the pack back in order anyway. Focus on that and your mating. We'll deal with getting Peter to a better place."

Russ was still talking when Everett pulled Peter up and guided him through the door. His cousin was completely out of it. Grey needed to hurry back. Everett dug through his pocket and found his cell phone, thankful he'd brought it with him. Grey was on speed dial.

"Hey, Ev, what's up? Is Pete okay? I've had this odd feeling—"

"That's why I'm calling. How close are you to the house?"

"We're close."

"Good, come to Kitty's when you get here."

"Pete?"

"Just get here, Grey."

"Fuck."

"Beyond fuck." Everett hung up, not giving Grey a chance to respond.

"Grey?" Peter whispered.

"It's okay, Petey, Grey will be here in no time."

"Okay. I need him, Ev."

"I know. I know. It'll be okay."

"Don—he wasn't joking, was he?" Peter stopped and Everett had no choice but to stop as well.

He turned Peter so they could look at each other. They were a bit away from the house now, and alone.

"No. He wasn't. What he did was wrong, but he's sorry."

"How can—"

"Just hear me out. Put yourself in his shoes. Your little brother comes out. You're thinking, this can't be bad. If he can do it, so can I. Then your dad responds like he does. What was Don supposed to do?"

"Stick up for me!" Peter's shout rang in Everett's ears.

"Me too, but Don isn't as strong as we are. Still, what he did was wrong and you don't ever have to forgive him."

"What about Dad? How is he—"

Oh, fuck.

Peter didn't know and now Everett was going to have to be the one to tell him. *Grey better hurry his ass up.*

"He hurt your mom pretty bad and I'm sorry, Peter, but he's…" How did someone tell a person that one of their parents was dead? Even if it was a bastard who deserved whatever he got. "Peter, your dad is dead. Don had to kill him. He went feral."

Everett waited to see Peter's response. Peter surprised him again by laughing. Not what he expected, but at least he wasn't catatonic.

Grey ran towards them. *Thank fuck.*

"Ev? Pete?" Grey looked confused.

"Don is here. He's the new alpha. Roger is dead."

"Why is he laughing?"

"I have no idea."

"He…he put Dad down. He…oh God." Peter rocked forward right into Grey's arms.

"Babe?" Grey stroked Peter's back.

"Sorry. Sorry. I'll be okay. I promise. A lot to process. A *lot*, but I have you and nothing else matters."

"That's right, Pete. Let's go home, okay? Thanks Ev."

"Any time. You know I'm here." Everett nodded.

He watched the mates walk away from him towards their own home. Now that the fire was out he could focus on getting settled in his own life. God, he needed to see Kitty. It was time to get his shit from his room and get moved into Kitty's place.

Chapter Ten

Kurt paced the room they'd locked him in. He needed to get out of the fucking pack house. How dare they try and contain him. Didn't they know who he was? He was a powerful important person and they'd made him look like a fool.

They'd pay. Fuckers were worried about exposure? He could fix that. All he needed to do was get out of the room. That shouldn't be too hard. He tugged at the door knob again, but it was locked. Kurt shoved his hands into his pocket and brushed them against something. It crinkled. Kurt took it out and to his surprise it was that magic dust that he'd picked up. One taste of that and nothing could stop him.

He was out of there. Once he had left he'd find someone to videotape him shifting and get it out to all of the news feeds. Then where would these pitiful people be? He'd make it so no one knew it was him undergoing the change and Kurt would make sure things pointed to the Masters pack.

Then he would play the outraged uncle, telling the news that a cult had taken his nieces. And hey — that changing thing on the television, he looked like the kidnapper. What was he going to do? Monsters had his family. That would take care of them all. He'd be the poor weeping uncle asking why this was happening to him.

It didn't matter that he'd never have Kitty. She was gone to him. He might have been able to manipulate her before, but things were different now and he wouldn't waste time getting rid of her like he had her parents.

Kurt would continue as the pack alpha and move up in the ranks of government. Maybe even take over where his brother left off.

First things first. Kurt opened the small bag and licked the contents. The zing of power almost overwhelmed him, but he was ready for shock. The first time it'd knocked him on his ass. The power built up in his system until he vibrated from the inside out, flooding his body, and he had to release power to get the edge off and make it easier to control.

He aimed his hands at the door and blew the thing clear off the hinges. The surprised look of the pup on the other side had him laughing.

"Hey! Sto—"

Kurt didn't give him time to finish. He pushed a bolt of magic into the shifter, waiting until the wolf didn't move before leaving the area. It was a great high. Kurt could see why people became addicted, but not him. After this last fix he wouldn't need it again.

When he had the Masters pack on the run, the satisfaction from that alone would be enough to sustain him.

There were no other obstacles between him and the front door. They had underestimated him and it would be the last mistake they made. Kurt stumbled against the wall. The power drain happened faster this time. He shook the bag. There was a bit left. He licked his finger and swished it around, getting as much of the powder as he could and sucking it off his digit. The zing wasn't as big this time, but he needed what he could get to leave the property without incident. Just a few more steps and he'd be home free. Once he cleared the steps, he'd shift. It would be easier to leave that way.

A blast from behind was unexpected, but he kept walking.

"Stop. Don't make me —"

Kurt turned and waved his hand, sending the poor schmuck who'd tried to stop him flying into the wall. The 'crash' as the shifter hit was very satisfying.

Finally he was at the door. He tugged his clothes off and shifted. He'd worry about clothes when he was closer to civilisation. The pack house really was off the beaten path. If he wasn't so pissed off, he might've admired Masters. Maybe. But now he wanted him dead.

Russell Masters had fucked with the wrong guy this time.

* * * *

What seemed like days had only been hours, when Kurt stopped at a motel. Being in wolf form did have its advantage for endurance, but running through the woods was not something he wanted to do on a daily basis. That was what the gym was for. He couldn't wait to get out of this backwater town.

The place looked deserted and he needed people — some fucking civilisation so he could be 'exposed'. He needed clothes and a camera. Kurt shifted back to human form and heard a gasp behind him. Just his luck there was a camera phone pointed his way. The stars were aligning in his favour.

The woman — if she could be called that, she looked all of thirteen — had a horrified expression on her face, her mouth gaping wide and her hands shaking. She hadn't screamed — yet.

"Miss, hand over your phone." Kurt held out his hand and made the 'give me' gesture.

"Please don't —"

"I'm not going to hurt you, you silly twit, unless you don't hand over the phone, then we might have a few issues. Now be a good girl and give it to me."

"What…what are you?"

"Just watch the news, darling, and everything will be explained. Now tell me, do you have a car?"

She nodded and pointed behind her. Kurt had missed it before, he'd been too focused on the motel.

"Good, good. Now what about some clothes?" Kurt grinned.

* * * *

Two hours later Kurt was on his way to D.C.. He had the perfect plan. He needed to get the phone into the hands of a reporter, but first he had to edit the video. It might not work. He still might need a reliable witness. He wasn't sure who he could trust. In the past he would have said Langford, but the bastard had betrayed him.

His brother had a few contacts who knew that werewolves existed and the Kelley family was made up of them, but would they leak the story? They had all been loyal to Arthur. They might think this was going against his wishes. He'd have to sweet-talk them somehow. Or maybe he could score some more magic dust and make them do what he wanted. That way seemed the easiest.

Bending people to his will was fun. Better than he could have possibly imagined.

Kurt would have plenty of time to think. He had no identification so he couldn't fly. It could pose a problem when the car ran out of gas. Kurt had to contact someone in D.C. to help him.

Then it hit him. He knew who would help him get what he wanted without exposing himself as a shifter. All arrows would point the Masters way by the time he was done. They'd be locked up for the greater good in no time flat. All ready to be examined and studied. It would serve them right for keeping Kitty away from him and brainwashing her into believing he was sick. He'd have to plan something wicked for the mate.

Who the fuck believed in that true mate shit anyway? So what if they performed the ritual. It didn't matter. If Kitty could be nice I might spare her. I'd have to keep her sisters on hand to keep her in line. She'd do anything for those whiny little bitches.

Kurt searched the interstate for the next gas station. He'd get off there and call his good pal who just happened to work for the Washington Post.

He'd looked at the video before he stole the car and the phone, the quality wasn't bad—for a cell, but Kurt's face was clearly visible and he didn't know much about manipulating it. He didn't want it to look fake, and he was afraid if he started doctoring it too much, people would notice that it had been messed with and call it bogus. Nope. He needed the real deal. A recording of him shifting. One where people couldn't see his face.

Plus he'd need gas soon and Dean, the reporter who was going to expose the shifters, owed him a few favours. Kurt wasn't above calling them all in. He also had a little blackmail on the good Dean. If the reporter stepped out of line, Kurt would call him to task.

It was all about the leverage and it was good that he had some. Kurt pulled off the highway. The sooner he got things in place the better. He knew he was racing against the clock. Kitty had contacts she could use, but Kurt didn't want to give her the time to tap them.

He *had* to beat her to the punch. Fear and a group of people went a long way because as a whole, people were stupid and prone to doing stupid things like forming lynch mobs. Just what he needed. Maybe he could talk Dean into filming him *at* the Masters pack house. That would be icing on the already delicious cake.

Now he was going to have to do some sweet talking. The gas station drew closer and closer, but he had no money. Maybe there would be change in the car he could use. He'd find out once he stopped. He should have picked a better car. The small smart car was anything but comfortable. His body was folding in all kinds of ways. He should have known better, but it was the only car around and he had to get this done — the sooner the better.

Kurt eased into the gas station and searched the car for loose change. He was in luck. Now he had to hope they had a payphone. Those things were a dying breed. If that failed, he'd have to ask the clerk to use the phone.

The whole situation was all kinds of wrong. He was one of the most prestigious lawyers in D.C. and here he was scrounging for change to make a stupid phone call. But what if Kitty had contacted someone already?

It was a possibility. From what he'd understood, the pack had been on high alert. It was pitch black outside and getting late. He should think about taking a nap too. The day only seemed to be getting longer. Dean might not even be up at this hour. Screw it. Kurt was calling him anyway. Time to put up or shut up and he was hoping for a put up.

He got out of the car to the most intoxicating smell. *What is that?* His cock got hard. It wasn't possible. He had control over his body. The scent got stronger the closer he got to the door. He hesitated before opening it.

"Good evening sir. Can I—" The clerk's eyes widened.

Kurt stopped dead in his tracks.

Mate.

Huh. So that was what it felt like. Kurt shrugged it off. It didn't matter in the greater scheme of things. Oh, but she smelt good.

"Hi. I'm Penny."

Kurt nodded. What was he going to do? He had to…expose shifters. Didn't he?

"I'm Kurt."

"Nice to meet you, Kurt. What brings you to my neck of the woods?" She smiled.

It made his heart ache, she was so gorgeous. Long blonde hair and twinkling brown eyes. She had dimples. Who knew he was a sucker for dimples? She'd asked him a question, but he was a bit lost.

His wolf whimpered. Kurt reined him in. *No. This wasn't what was supposed to happen. I have a mission.*

"I—" Kurt began.

A voice whispered in his head. *Let the past go and all can be forgiven. Continue on your path and you will be destroyed.*

Kurt cocked his head. Who was—oh, fuck. The Ancients? He thought they were a myth, but he wouldn't have told himself to stop seeking revenge.

"You okay?" She was still smiling.

"I'm good, Penny. Actually, better than I've ever been."

Chapter Eleven

Kitty wondered what was taking Ev so long. How much stuff could one man have in one of those dorm-style rooms? She looked around her place. It really had become home to her and the girls. She missed her parents, but not the lifestyle they'd lived. It wasn't one she'd ever coveted. Here in the woods, it was peaceful.

"Hey, stop fretting. Did your man run off? You should totally go for a girl. They don't run." Poppy threw herself down on the couch and bit into an apple.

She shook her head. "Where's Bunny?"

"In her room."

"Could you get her please?"

"Bunny!" Poppy yelled without getting up, bits of apple spraying out of her mouth.

"I could have done that and you need to clean that up. Talking with food in your mouth is disgusting, yelling with it is even worse."

"Then you should have." Poppy grinned, took another bite and opened her mouth wide.

Never a dull moment with the twins around.

Bunny came into the room and plopped down beside her sister, taking the apple from her and eating some.

"We need to talk."

"Oh no, what did Bunny do now?" Poppy pinched her sister's side.

"Me? Why does it have to be me?" Bunny glared and rubbed at the spot her sister had hurt.

"I'm not the one Kitty yelled for."

"No, because you were already here." Bunny pouted.

"Still—what did you do, sis?" Poppy winked.

"Both of you stop." Kitty paced in front of them, rubbing her forehead. "Neither of you did anything. There are a couple of things we need to discuss. First—Mom and Dad." Kitty stopped and looked at them.

She hated to bring it up. It was a sore topic for all of them, but the girls should be aware of the truth.

"I don't wanna." Bunny curled up into Poppy.

The twins held onto each other like a lifeline. Kitty didn't want to talk about it either, but they needed to know.

"None of us do, Bunny. But you need to know— what I thought happened, well—it didn't."

"What do you mean?" Poppy frowned.

"Mom didn't kill Dad or herself. Well—technically, yes, but it was Uncle Kurt. He…there was some magic involved and he forced it on them. He killed our parents." Kitty bit her lip and waited for a response.

"Where's Kurt now?" Bunny had tears in her eyes. Despite the earlier bickering, Poppy stroked her sister's hair.

"They have him sequestered on the property somewhere. I didn't ask where."

"Good. That's good. He can't...hurt us, can he?" Poppy looked nervous.

She hated this—the fact that someone had the power to make them this uncomfortable. She wouldn't stand for it. They were home and Kurt wasn't going to ruin that for them.

"No. Russ will make sure that we are safe. I trust him. This is our home and we won't be run out of it. Got it? We're here to stay. Which brings me to the other thing I need to talk to you guys about...Everett."

Poppy snorted. At least she didn't look so scared anymore. Bunny giggled. There. That was what she wanted, the easy-going girls she loved. They didn't cower anymore after their brief stay with the Tyler pack.

"He's moving in today. I know I should have talked to you both, but he is my mate and I...well, I want him with me."

"Oh...gag. Really? You won't be all lovey-dovey, right? For all that is holy, please—no kissing in the living room. Or the kitchen. We have to eat there." Poppy made a retching sound.

Bunny grabbed her sister and tackled her to the floor, covering her mouth with her hands.

"Don't listen to her, Kitty." Bunny 'oomphed'. Poppy elbowed her, but she continued. "She's just jealous because she doesn't have a girl right now. It's—hey, no biting!" Bunny licked the side of Poppy's face and giggled some more. "It's really great and if you want...well—" Bunny bit her lip. "We could move to the big house."

Poppy's eyes widened and she stopped struggling. Both girls were serious now. They sat up with their backs to the couch.

"No. Not happening. We're a family and we'll figure it out." Kitty went to them and sat on the floor, wriggling in between them, hugging them close.

"What if Everett doesn't like us?"

"How could that be possible?"

"Poppy is kind of a brat."

Kitty hurried up and moved out of striking range. She knew where it was going and no way was she getting in the middle of it. Thankfully, a knock at the door gave her an out. "You two—don't break anything." Kitty pointed a finger at them and gave them a mock scowl before heading to the door.

"Hey."

She smiled. It was Ev. He was back. "Hey."

"Sorry it took so long. There was…an issue."

Kitty searched his face. His eyes looked tense and his mouth drooped—almost…sad.

Kitty held out a hand and brought him into the house. "What's wrong?"

She steered him towards the kitchen and heard a thud from the direction of the living room.

"Should I be worried?" Everett looked behind him, but Kitty kept moving.

"They won't hurt each other." An 'ouch' from one of the girls had her amending her answer. "Much, they won't hurt each other much. So, tell me, what happened." Kitty pushed Ev into a chair and made herself busy with some coffee. She needed some caffeine and it was her drug of choice. She could drink it all day long.

"Don is here. I guess he's the new alpha of the Tyler pack. He…he had to kill Roger. Pete came in while we were talking. Get this…Don is gay."

Kitty dropped the coffee and turned. "No way. Not after…how…"

"Guess he's been closeted up. Once Pete came out he thought he had no choice and he took his anger out on his brother. I met Don's mate, Lincoln. Seems nice. I'm not sure if Pete will ever forgive him. It's a mess. Grey came and took Pete back to their place. So…yeah, that's why I'm late. What's up with the war zone in your living room?"

The girls were still at it. Kitty'd have to put a stop to it soon or something would get broken and with their luck it would be a bone and not the couch.

"I told them about Mom and Dad. Then I told them you were moving in."

"I don't have to." Everett looked so serious.

Kitty walked over to him and straddled his lap. "Yes." She kissed his chin. "You do." Kitty brushed her lips against his.

She was lost in the kiss. A gagging noise brought her out of it.

"I said not in the kitchen. Geez, now I'll never be able to eat here again." Poppy crossed her arms and glared at them.

Everett chuckled. At least the mood was lightened. Before she could address Poppy her phone rang. She watched the girls sit at the table and start talking to Everett. They could totally make this work.

"Hello."

"Hello. Is this Kitty Kelley?"

"Yes it is, may I ask who is calling?"

"This is Patricia Sparks' secretary. You left a message for the First Lady yesterday and I was returning your call. She has a few minutes to speak to you."

"Thank you. Yes, please."

"Hold for the First Lady."

That was fast. Kitty hadn't expected a call so soon. She figured the senator would have got back to her first.

"Kitty? This is Patricia. Bobbie said you needed to speak to me."

"Patricia. It's wonderful to hear from you. Yes. I have...an issue that I think your husband needs to hear about. It's important or I wouldn't be bothering you."

"I wanted to say I'm sorry about your parents. It was an awful day. I wanted to express my condolences personally, but you'd disappeared. Does this matter have anything to do with your leaving Washington?"

"Yes, it does." Kitty took a deep breath. "I know this is going to sound crazy, but I'm not. This is something serious. Have you heard of shifters?"

"You mean, like in movies and television shows? I really don't have time to watch those. But, yes, I've heard of them."

"They're real."

"Kitty, I know the loss of your parents in such a horrific way could scar anyone, but—"

Kitty interrupted her, "This isn't about my parents. I assure you. I'm not making stuff up or trying to get attention. If I was, I would have stayed in D.C. and caused a stir. We both know I could have. We are about to be exposed. My alpha needs to talk to the President so we don't cause a nationwide panic. There are a few senators my father was friends with who know the truth."

"This...Kitty, how can—?"

"It's off-the-wall strange. I know that. Just—if you could get us an appointment with your husband, my alpha could explain it better. I'm not sure when the exposure will happen, but if it does before we release a statement, things could be really, really bad."

"He isn't going to believe…"

"He'll have to once we show him. It would be me, the alpha and his wife, plus one more. Just a nice sit-down meeting."

There was a pause. Kitty waited for the First Lady to hang up on her.

"Your dad was a good man. For him, I'll get you a meeting, but Kitty, if this is—"

"It isn't. I promise. Thank you."

"Get here today and I'll get you in to see him."

"Thank you."

The First Lady hung up. Kitty put her phone down. She'd been so focused on the call she hadn't heard her sisters and Ev behind her. They were close. Kitty walked towards Ev and he opened his arms for her.

"That sounded promising." Ev stroked her back.

"It was. We need to let Russ know and make our way to Washington." Kitty rubbed her cheek against Ev's chest.

"Before you leave, Poppy and I wanted to say— we're happy for you two and are good to go for Everett moving in."

"I don't know about this good to go stuff, but yeah. It's cool." Poppy winked and sauntered out of the room.

Kitty closed her eyes and smiled. Her sister might give her a hard time, but that was all a show. She hoped her sisters found their mates and could be happy—well—in a few years. College first.

"We should—" Kitty started, but Ev stopped her.

He pressed his lips to hers and slid his tongue against her lips. Kitty let him in and jumped, wrapping her legs around his stomach. Everett was so strong.

"Guys—don't you have somewhere to be?" A yell from the other room broke them apart.

She couldn't tell if it was Poppy or Bunny, but they were right. Kitty released Ev and hugged him tight.

"They're right. Let's go talk to Russ and then maybe we can get the girls to give us a bit of time alone later."

"I like that idea." Ev held out his hand.

Kitty took it and let him lead her to the front door.

Bunny stopped them. "Hey, a friend of ours asked if we could stay over. You know—cards and talk. All that fun. It's here on the compound so—"

"Okay. That would be great. Do you need anything?"

"No. We'll probably be gone by the time you get back."

"All right. Call if you need something and…no sex!"

"Kitty!" Bunny looked outraged.

"Don't 'Kitty' me. I was your age not long ago."

"Whatever. Just…go."

"I'll probably be in D.C. later. You guys will be okay, right? I'll let the others know."

"Stop worrying. We can stay with the Loys as long as we need to. And their parents will be there. Nothing will happen." Poppy rolled her eyes.

Kitty gave them both a hug before Ev tugged her away.

"I don't want to come between you guys." Ev sounded worried.

"You won't. You'll just add to the family fun." Kitty grinned.

"Fun, huh? Yeah, never a dull moment. We'll have to let Pete and Grey look after them for a bit when we get back. I'd love to see Pete's face when Bunny goes all gooey-eyed with him."

"Yep, you'll fit right in." Kitty laughed.

There was a commotion at the house when they arrived.

"What's going on?" Everett stopped one of the pack members.

"Kurt escaped."

"What!" This couldn't be happening. "The girls—"

"You go talk to Russ, I'll go get the girls." Everett rushed out the door.

She had to calm herself. Ev would take care of her sisters and she'd go talk to Russ about meeting the commander-in-chief. Kurt wasn't their only worry. Kitty stood up straight and headed for Russ. She was ready for normal. Whatever that was.

Chapter Twelve

"The President. I can't believe we're going to meet him." Everett looked around the plane.

"The Ancients were right, Kitty, you and Everett are the key." Russ glanced over at them. His mate Vivian was beside him.

"Not me, but Kitty for sure."

Kitty just shrugged. She'd been preoccupied. Not that he blamed her. They had the girls safe. They couldn't have them staying with another shifter family. Grey was a protector so they'd stashed the girls with Peter and Grey. He'd only been half kidding when he said the girls should stay with them, but he was happy they had that option. Now they could focus on the shifter problem. Hopefully the others would find Kurt before he caused any damage. There had been no trace of him on the pack grounds. He could've been anywhere by now, which he knew had Kitty on edge.

They were on a commercial flight. They had their own plane, but it was easier to just buy tickets. Too much red tape involved in landing in D.C..

"I just had a number."

Vivian laughed. They were all in one row of four. Kitty and Vivian were in the middle leaving the ends for Russ and Ev.

"Just a number? We're talking the First Lady here. That is more than some digits." Russ shook his head.

Everett took Kitty's hand and kissed her palm. "It'll be okay. The girls are safe. We'll be back in no time."

"Thank you for coming."

"I wouldn't be anywhere else." Everett assured her.

And he wouldn't. He belonged at her side.

Kitty laid her head on his shoulder. "And I wouldn't have you anywhere else. I just wish…I want…normal, you know?"

"I do know. Hopefully we'll get the reveal out of the way and we can all settle down."

"It won't happen that way. We'll be freaks and there will be reporters and —"

"Maybe at first. But that will die down eventually and we can think about us. We might have to get a few more guards for the house, but other than that, we're good."

"He's right, Kitty. Things will calm down once people get used to the fact that shifters are real and here to stay. There will be some that will always oppose our existence, but we'll ignore them and continue to live our lives." Russ leaned over in his seat to look into Kitty's eyes.

Everett felt her calming down beside him. It was that damn alpha voice. Russ had that effect on all of them. Hopefully it would work on the President.

Before he knew it, they were landing. They'd each only brought an overnight bag so they didn't have to go to the baggage claim area. Kitty had called Langford to arrange a ride. They were going right to the White House so they'd be ready when the President was.

To his surprise, Langford himself waited beside a car.

"I thought I'd go with you." Langford opened the door for Vivian. She slid in, Russ behind her.

"Have you heard from Kurt?" Kitty rubbed her arms.

Everett noticed she'd stopped calling him uncle.

"No, I haven't. I figured he'd be back trying to take over, by force if necessary. I have guards out. Are you ready?" Langford gestured for them to get in the vehicle.

"Yes. I never thought I'd be back here."

"You don't have to come back after this is all over," Everett assured her.

They got in and sped along the streets.

* * * *

Langford parked the car. Everett hated the city with all the traffic and smog. The noises were too much. He preferred the quiet of the pack house. The drive to the White House seemed to take forever. No one really wanted to talk on the drive and that was fine with him.

He kept glancing at Kitty to make sure she was okay. He knew she didn't want to be here. She'd left this life behind and now they were dragging her back into it. Once this was settled he'd get her back to where she'd finally become comfortable.

Kitty gave him a small smile and took his hand.

"You'll want to leave everything in the car except for ID. It'll go easier that way. As it is, we'll have to wait a bit to clear security." Langford got out of the car.

"Why? They know we're coming." Everett was confused.

"Yes, they know, but there are still protocols in place. You can't just waltz into the place. They'll want our identification. Then they will compare them to the paperwork I submitted earlier today. As it is, we are being a bit rushed through. It's unheard of to get in to see the President on the same day you fill out your security information. That is thanks to the First Lady. If not for Kitty and her family we wouldn't even be able to get up to the doors." Langford helped Kitty from the car.

"Seems a bit much." Everett shrugged.

"It's also the President of the United States. He needs to be protected. You'll also be frisked so don't go all wolf on the Secret Service agents." Langford gave a pointed glare towards Everett.

Like I'd be the one — okay, I probably would. I'll have to be extra careful.

They reached the doors and were stopped by security, and sure enough, they had to stand there as each of their IDs were copied. The head, or he assumed it was the head, of security talked into the walkie-talkie on his shoulder. There was some back and forth until — a half hour later they were let in. They were stopped multiple times along the way, but weren't frisked again. *Thank goodness.* After the first time he needed a bath. Kitty rubbed his back, as if she knew he was tense. *Maybe I shouldn't have come. I could be a liability.*

He didn't belong in this world. But, man, Kitty did. She was in her element. She looked a little — royal. And she was all his.

"This shouldn't take long. I hope." Kitty squeezed his bicep.

The guard led them to a sitting area. "The President's secretary will let you know when you can go in."

They were left in the room. Everett wondered how much more waiting they would have to do. He looked down at what he was wearing—jeans and a T-shirt. He was so underdressed. He should have changed, but they were in a hurry. *God, who met the President in jeans?* Not Russ or Langford. They looked nice in their casual wear. Even the ladies were nicely attired. *Fuck.*

"You okay?" Russ put a hand on his arm to stop Everett from pacing.

He was getting agitated and he needed to stop. He couldn't screw things up. This was big.

A tall striking woman stood in the doorway. "The President will see you now." She turned as if expecting them to follow. They moved single file out of the room until they were shown into a sitting area similar to the one they'd just left.

The President had his back to them. He looked regal—more so in real life than on TV.

"Sir, your guests are here."

President Sparks turned and smiled at them.

"Kitty. So sorry about your family. My wife was a bit mysterious as to the meeting, saying you'd show me. My curiosity is getting the better of me."

"Thank you, sir. Yes. It will be a bit hard to believe, but—I'm sure you'll understand in a moment."

Two Secret Service men stood in the background. They tried to be invisible, but if Everett wasn't mistaken, one was a were. He wondered if he was from Kitty's pack.

"Have a seat." The President motioned them to chairs.

"Let me make introductions. This is my alpha Russ Masters and his mate Vivian. My mate Everett and you know me, well, maybe of me, I'm not sure we've ever really met."

"No, but my wife has always spoken highly of you and of course, I was close to your father."

"Yes, well, I'm going to let Russ explain why we're here."

Everett wondered if the President was paying attention to the words Kitty used. 'Mate' and 'alpha' weren't words most threw around in everyday conversation.

"Sir, it's a pleasure to meet you, but I'm afraid we are here because something big is about to happen. I am a wolf shifter and my mate is a fox shifter." Russ paused for effect, but the President didn't even flinch.

"Ah, so this is about exposure."

"You don't seem too shocked." Russ leant back in his chair.

"No, Mr Masters, I'm not. I've been privy to your existence for a while."

Kitty gasped. "My dad, he told you, didn't he?"

"He did. He felt I would be better protected with a few of his pack as my security after the last assassination attempt. I admit, I wasn't as calm the first time." President Sparks winked at Kitty. "What can I do for you?"

This was unexpected, but a good thing. It would have been harder if not for Kitty and the fact that the news wasn't a shock.

"I have a reporter in my pack who's going to do a human interest piece on shifters. It would be great if you could make a statement to the people letting them know we aren't a threat and then we can air our piece.

Valerie only had a few more interviews to do and she'll be ready."

"Consider it done. How is tomorrow night? That will give me time to prepare something and for your person to finish up. My camp will want to pre-screen the video before it goes live, of course."

"Yes, of course and we would like to see your speech before it goes live," Russ countered.

"Very good. We'll get that arranged. Give my secretary your email address and she'll give you mine." The President stood and their group followed suit. "Now, I have a few things to get out of the way so I can work on what I'm going to say. I hope to hear more from you Mr Masters. Kitty." The President pulled her into a hug. "Don't be a stranger."

And with that the man was gone. One of the security team went with him and the other stayed behind.

"Is it true, we're going to be exposed?"

"Yes. And you're?" Russ held out a hand.

"Sorry. Brett Manning. I'm part of Kitty—well, I guess it's Langford's pack now."

"We have a seer in our pack and the Ancients gave her a vision of a news story breaking and news reel of a shifter mid shift. It could be explained away, but it is time for us to come out, so to speak."

"Are you sure this is a good idea, sir?"

"No, but I want a safe future for our children. If we take care of this now, by the time the young are old enough, it will be old news."

"Just let us know how we can help." Brett left as well.

"Okay, let's get out of here. I need to get a status update from Valerie. Let me exchange email addresses and we'll head home. Our return flight"—Russ looked down at his watch—"doesn't leave for a bit. We have time for some lunch first."

They were outside the car when someone stopped beside Kitty. Everett turned and grabbed his mate, putting her behind him.

"Wait. Wait. I need help." Kurt slouched against the car and ran a hand through his hair.

He looked different from before—defeated and more haggard. Something had to have happened between his escape and now to put the look of utter dejection on his face.

"What do you want, Kurt?" Russ finally came out of the White House.

"I need help. I was…wrong."

"What happened?" Russ raised an eyebrow.

"I met my mate."

"Ah, you do know you will never be an alpha of a pack again. You should probably find a new pack and I might have the one for you, if you don't cause problems. You stay away from us and Kitty and I'll get you the help you need. Now if you'll excuse us, we have places to be." Russ nodded and got into the car.

"I'm sorry, Kitty," Kurt whispered the words. If Everett hadn't been standing so close he wouldn't have heard.

"I can't accept that, Kurt. You killed my parents no matter the technicalities. It was your fault." Kitty patted Everett's back and climbed into the backseat, leaving him alone with Kurt.

"You stay away from my family or you'll die. Do we understand each other?" Everett waited for Kurt to acknowledge him before he too got into the vehicle. He turned to look out the window. Kurt stared at the ground and didn't move. His shoulders were slumped and if it was anyone else, Everett might have felt sorry for him. As it was, he felt cheated out of ripping Kurt a new one.

"You okay, Kitty?"

She nodded, but was silent. Everett would feel better when they got home. They might never know what drove Kurt to the point he had the need to kill his brother and his wife and Everett didn't really care. He had his girls to take care of now. He hugged Kitty close and kissed her head. Home had never sounded so good.

Chapter Thirteen

"People of this great nation, I have an announcement to make. One that some of you will not be prepared for. Over the next few days I want you to really think about your response to my news. After I am finished you will see a few interviews. I urge you all to watch them so you can have a better understanding of what is taking place.

"Shifters are real. This is not a joke. It isn't April Fools or even a prank. No, you are not being 'Punk'd'. I have met a few wolf shifters in my day and have just been introduced to a lovely fox shifter. They are not freaks or monsters. They are just like you and me. The only difference is they can change into different animals.

"I want you to respect them for the humans that they are. Do not go out searching for these people. Leave them to lead their lives as they see fit. I will not stand for hate crimes against shifters anymore than I stand for any kind of hate. My staff will be taking calls if you have any questions. Now I'll leave you to watch the interviews of a few shifters who were willing to open their lives to you."

The screen faded. Kitty and the rest of the pack watched in the theatre room as the President of the United States told the world of their existence. It was tense in the room, as was to be expected. No one wanted to go public, but you listened when the Ancients spoke, at least that was what she'd learned since coming to the Masters pack.

Next up were Bella and David. They looked so—normal. She had no idea what to expect. They hadn't been shown the video beforehand. She was just happy she hadn't needed to be interviewed.

"Hello, my name is Bella and this is my mate, David. We're shifters." Bella placed a hand on her stomach. "As you can see we're about to become parents. I'm excited and a bit nervous. We just found out we're having triplets. Not what we were expecting, but we're happy all the same."

A voice from off camera spoke. "How did you and David meet?"

"I went searching for her and brought her to our pack house," David answered.

"Pack house?" the voice asked.

Kitty knew it was Valerie, but it was a bit disconcerting not seeing her on camera.

"Yes, we have an alpha, a man who is in charge of all of us. Keeps us in line." David grinned. "We live together because just like real wolves we like to be in big groups. It's just easier when we have a head to take charge. It's also like one big family, only not just on holidays."

"Now, you shift. Is this something you control?" Valerie asked.

"Yes. The urge might be a bit stronger on a full moon, but for the most part I can control it. If I'm extremely emotional it can be difficult. That is why we homeschool our young. The little ones have more difficulty controlling it at first and need help. Sometimes they'll stay in wolf form for days before figuring out how to shift back. Would you like me to show you?" David stood. He started to take off his shirt and shoes. He left his pants on.

Probably a good thing since they weren't airing this on cable. David's shift was flawless. Sure, some might say it was staged and people would be examining the footage for ages to come.

David stayed in wolf form. Bella petted him. She smiled at her mate.

The scene changed to Peter and Grey. Peter kept glancing at the door like he wanted to be anywhere, but in that room. Grey held his hand tightly, as if he was trying to keep Peter in his seat.

"Please, Peter, Greycen, tell us a bit about how you met."

"Grey came to the house looking for his sister. I—I wasn't ready for a mate, but some things you can't argue with."

"Why weren't you ready, Peter?"

"I was told—" He looked at Grey who nodded. "I was told I would never have a mate because gay men didn't have them. I was an abomination."

"So you have the same issues as a shifter as other homosexuals?"

"Yes, we do. There isn't much different between a shifter and a full human. We have the same problems. Peter was tossed out of his pack and found our current home. I wasn't going to let him go. Not once I found him."

"Why is that?" Valerie asked.

"When wolves find their mates, they know. It's instinctual. We're born with another half and it hurts once you find it and can't be with the other person. It took some convincing, but finally Peter came around."

"And your alpha, he's fine with this?"

"Yes. He knows how mating works. We don't pick. When our destined mate shows up the urge to be one is strong." Grey glanced over at Peter.

The love could be felt through the screen. Kitty could see how much they meant to each other. It was how her sisters told her she stared at Everett. Everett stood and tugged Kitty up with him. She saw him wink at the girls before he led Kitty out of the room.

Someone else was talking, but her focus was now on her mate. They walked to their home. She loved how that sounded – theirs.

"Don't you want to watch the other interviews? Valerie did a great job."

"Nope." He kept tugging her along. They reached the door and he opened it, still dragging her. They didn't stop until they reached their bedroom.

Everett locked the door. Kitty just stood and watched as he pulled his clothes off. He was naked in a matter of seconds. If she had blinked, Kitty would have missed it.

"One of us is wearing too many clothes." Everett looked at her expectantly.

Right. Too many clothes. She took her time, peeling one article off, then another, before wriggling out of her underwear. Both of them stood and stared at each other.

"Now one of us is too far away." Kitty smiled.

He pounced. Good thing they were close to the bed. They tumbled into it with Kitty ending up under Ev.

His weight pushed her into the bed. She was in heaven. Kitty closed her eyes and enjoyed the sensations. Ev sucked at her neck, nibbling on her ear lobe. He kissed his way down her body, stopping only to flick her nipples with his tongue. They'd never been particularly sensitive, but something about Ev had her arching her back and wanting more. He bit down into it before soothing the nipple. Kitty dug her heels into the mattress and rubbed against Ev's cock. She wanted that inside her in the worst way, but Ev was in no hurry. He gave her other breast the same treatment before moving along. His next stop was her belly button. It tickled when he licked inside. This was fun. He made foreplay a big deal. She wasn't some innocent, but no one had ever made her feel the way Ev did. He nuzzled his nose into her pussy, just breathing on her, and it drove her insane. Kitty rocked against him, but Ev held her hips down.

"I'm not rushing this, Kitty."

God, even having him talk against her was a turn-on. She bucked up.

"Don't make me tie you up."

Kitty groaned.

"Oh, I see someone likes that idea. We'll explore it — later. For now —"

Ev stroked her long and hard.

"Ev — please, I need —"

He didn't say anything, just moved to her opening and fucked her with his tongue. He used his thumb to rub her slit. Ev used his other thumb and circled her asshole. He eased his thumb inside and she came apart, screaming his name. Ev moved up her body and slid his cock into her pussy. She was already clutching around him. It was like her orgasm went on and on, no end in sight.

No rush on his part, but she was going crazy. Ev kept his strokes slow and steady, pressing her down in the bed. She wrapped her legs around his hips, using her feet to push him in harder, but he wouldn't cooperate. Ev nibbled at her lips and pinched her nipples. All of the sensations were too much.

"Too much. Ev—please, please." She thrashed her head back and forth against the pillow.

"Shh, shhh," he murmured against her lips.

How can he even think right now? Kitty scratched down his back and met him stroke for stroke until he lost his rhythm.

"Come for me. Please, please—I want—need…" She couldn't even form a complete sentence.

Her climax was building, if it ever stopped. Her body flew apart.

"Kitty, Kitty…close."

She wrapped tighter around him, clutching him to her. They screamed together. Kitty came so hard she would've sworn she saw stars.

It was a few minutes before she could even think again, much less speak. The silence was nice. Who knew what the future would bring, but at this moment she was right where she needed to be—surrounded by friends and family.

"I know this is too soon, but I have to say it. I love you, Kitty. You were born to be mine." Ev hugged her close to his side.

"It is too soon, but I feel it too, Ev. My soul is at peace and I didn't think that would ever happen in this lifetime. You make me feel loved and safe. Something I've needed for a while now."

"I've needed it too. When Peter met Grey and I watched them struggle, I swore I'd never let my mate go. I'd give you all the time you need, but you were mine."

"No, that doesn't sound creepy at all." Kitty laughed.

"Well…now that I think about it." Ev leered at her.

"Who are you kidding? That was some of the best sex of my life, there is no way I could go another round."

"Are you challenging me again?"

Kitty laughed. "I know better than to challenge you."

She moved her head so she could stare into his eyes. Contentment washed over her.

Who knew what the humans would bring, but she would take Ev's earlier advice and live her life for the moment, not worry about what might happen.

"Man, are you guys at it *again*?"

That could only be Poppy, pitching her voice loud enough so they could hear it through the closed door.

There was whispering that Kitty didn't catch.

"Maybe we need a bigger place." Ev shook his head.

"What, and miss the comedy hour of the Kelley sisters?" Kitty tickled Ev.

He tried to wiggle away, but she was relentless. They were both breathless and laughing when they heard Bunny this time.

"We're going back to the big house. Call us when you're ready for us to come home."

The door closed, leaving them alone again. Kitty wondered what Bunny had bribed Poppy with to get her out of the house. She'd worry about that—maybe later. Way later. She had a mate to enjoy. Let whatever happened come, she'd be ready to deal with it, but not alone. Never alone again.

Epilogue

Sometime in the near future

The widespread panic over the reveal of the shifters had died down. The Ancients were happy with the outcome. They knew their wolves would do the right thing if steered in the direction they needed to go. The Ancients looked over to where it all started—well, at least in this century. The couple who had got the ball rolling on the greatest prophecy they'd ever had or would have—David and Bella Sanders. Their triplets were babies no more. One stood out. She was tall like her mother with the same red hair and green eyes. She would be the one they talked to in the future. Not that they'd need to guide the pack again for some time to come.

Rogue, Parker and Josey—the Sanders triplets— played with their friends Rose, Erin and Scott's little girl. There was much laughter in the park where they frolicked. Rogue tilted her head and the Ancients sent out a feeling of love and peace before leaving them to play and be children.

In Valerie and Max Rockwell's home there was a fight going on. Two little boys, Henry and Richard, tugged a doll between them. Valerie came into the room looking very pregnant. She took the doll and slapped both boys on the head, sending them to their room muttering something about hoping the next one was a girl and it was all Max's fault. The Ancients knew for a fact that it was another boy, but they would let Valerie figure it out for herself. There was no need for whispers in her direction. Valerie would handle the boys like everything else in her life, with dignity and a lot of questions.

The next stop took them to the little grotto the wolves seemed to like to spend time in. Russ and Vivian watched their little girl, Roberta, shift for the first time. She would be their only child and doted upon by her parents and the rest of the pack—a little princess who would go on to lead the foxes. There was great promise in the girl and they would watch with interest as she grew into a powerful woman. The magical power that Russ lacked was made up for in his daughter. Not only that, but Roberta could shift into both a fox and a wolf—something that hadn't been heard of until now. There would be more mixed species who would do the same, but Roberta was special and the first of her kind.

Zareb and Joy relaxed in bed. They didn't stay long with the couple. The Ancients didn't like to peek in when their children shared carnal knowledge. At least most of them didn't. Joy and Zareb would be blessed with children, but not for a while. Zareb was needed to help guide Roberta. Plus, Zareb deserved all the time he needed to be with his love. They'd put him through enough in his lifetime. He needed the peace his mate brought him. Joy started to stroke Zareb and it was time to leave.

Djimon. He was the one they worried about the most. Even they couldn't predict everything. There was too much choice involved for a finite future. It could have gone so wrong so many different ways. But Ive had come along just in time. She was what he needed. Someone with such passion. They too were childless—but not for long. Ive didn't know it yet, but she was with child. She would make a wonderful and protective mother. The couple were on their way to meet Ive's brother Greycen and his partner Peter. There was the matter of some adoption papers to sign. The two were about to become daddies. Peter wasn't sure at first, but Grey and Ive talked him into it. They would make fine fathers for the poor orphaned shifter. That was the way of life. Others died so more could live.

Things were better between Peter and his brother Don. Lincoln was a big help in getting the brothers to talk. He and Grey had become fast friends. Don was growing into his leadership role and nothing like his father as he'd feared. Don and Lincoln didn't want children, but would be doting uncles. There would be more than one child in Peter and Grey's future.

Kir and his mate Naomi were currently running in wolf form around the property. Another one of their children they'd worried about. Kir was settling in nicely to his new home. He was also a surprise to them—someone who became more important because of his choices. He, Zareb and Djimon would be the backbone of the tribe teaching the pack the old ways— letting more than just the Masters pack become more spiritual. Too much had been lost and not enough knew about the Ancients guiding their lives. Kir and

Naomi would never have children of their own, but the couple would be happy with it that way. There were so many pups running around the Masters pack now that they would always have children around.

Soon, Kir and Naomi would travel to the other packs and teach them the ways of the Ancients. They were proud, as proud as they could be of their creations.

Pups—in a property on the outskirts of the pack there two pups chased two children. Everett and Kitty's children, the four of them. Two sets of twins. They were all excited about their uncle Peter bringing home a new friend they could play with. Their aunts were on babysitting duty. Everett and Kitty were running behind, but they were going to be there when Peter and Grey officially became parents. Everett wouldn't miss it.

There were still some rumbling about shifters being among humans. There was nothing the Ancients could do about it. For now there was a well-deserved peace over the Masters tribe.

There had been many trials, but the Masters knew how to navigate them to their best ability. The Ancients were happy with the way the events had played out.

"Sister, what are you doing?"

"I'm watching over our children."

"They are fine, sister. Leave them be."

The world view through the clouds closed as she left their children to their own devices.

After all, there was a time when a parent had to let go. They would need them again and the Ancients would always have an ear open to their children for any trials they may have, but now—now was time to rejoice in the beauty of life, knowing they'd played a little part in making so many people happy.

A voice broke through the clouds.

"Thank you, Ancients, for my family and finally some peace."

She peeked to see Everett looking towards the heaven with a smile on his face. She pushed through her happiness and finally went about her day to see what other trouble might need attending—somewhere far, far away from the Masters.

About the Author

Jambrea wanted to be the youngest romance author published, but life impeded the dreams. She put her writing aside and went to college briefly, then enlisted in the Air Force. After serving in the military, she returned home to Indiana to start her family. A few years later, she discovered yahoo groups and book reviews. There was no turning back. She was bit by the writing bug.

She enjoys spending time with her son when not writing and loves to receive reader feedback. She's addicted to the internet so feel free to email her anytime.

Jambrea Jo Jones loves to hear from readers. You can find her contact information, website details and author profile page at http://www.total-e-bound.com.

Total-E-Bound Publishing

www.total-e-bound.com

Take a look at our exciting range of literagasmic™
erotic romance titles and discover pure quality
at Total-E-Bound.

Total-E-Bound Publishing books by Jambrea Jo Jones:

Alliance Volume One
Retribution
Salvation

Alliance Volume One
Freedom
Reward

Seeds of Dawn Volume One
Dreams
Secrets

Seeds of Dawn Volume Two
Inequities
Origins

Dark Encounters
Dominate Me
Feel Me

Semper Fi
Magnus
Ben

Love by Design
Wishing Star
Stealing Michael
Tell Me Now
A Fistful of Emmett
Rayne's Wild Ride
Operation Get Spencer